"Would you do me a favor?"

Dylan's deep voice rolled over her. "You certainly aren't backward about asking for what you want—I'll give you that."

"I need you to get the key for my cuffs."

After a long, slow pause he said, "The key?"

She squeezed her eyes more tightly shut. "It's in my top right breast pocket. I can't reach it. So, unless you do want me to become a permanent fixture…"

The rest of her words dried up in her throat and her eyes flung open.

It seemed she hadn't had to ask twice. Dylan's hand was already sliding into the pocket, his fingertips brushing against the soft cotton over her bra—just slowly enough so that a ripple of goosebumps sprang up all over her body, and just fast enough so that she couldn't accuse him of taking advantage.

All too soon he held up the key. "This the one you're after?"

She hoped to God it was. If he made another foray in there she didn't know what she might do.

What do you look for in a guy? Charisma. Sex appeal. Confidence. A body to die for. Looks that stand out from the crowd. Well, look no further—the heroes in this miniseries have all this, and more! And now that they've met the women in these novels, there is one thing on everyone's mind....

NIGHTS *of* PASSION

One night is never enough!

These guys know what they want and how they're going to get it!

Don't miss any of these hot stories, where romance and sizzling passion are guaranteed!

Ally Blake

GETTING RED-HOT WITH THE ROGUE

NIGHTS *of* PASSION

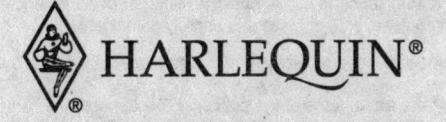

HARLEQUIN®

TORONTO • NEW YORK • LONDON
AMSTERDAM • PARIS • SYDNEY • HAMBURG
STOCKHOLM • ATHENS • TOKYO • MILAN • MADRID
PRAGUE • WARSAW • BUDAPEST • AUCKLAND

Recycling programs
for this product may
not exist in your area.

ISBN-13: 978-0-373-12874-7

GETTING RED-HOT WITH THE ROGUE

First North American Publication 2009.

www.eHarlequin.com

Printed in U.S.A.

All about the author...
Ally Blake

When **ALLY BLAKE** was a little girl, she made a wish that when she turned twenty-six she would marry an Italian two years older than herself. After it actually came true, she realized she was on to something with these wish things. So, next she wished that she could make a living spending her days in her pajamas, eating M&M's and drinking scads of coffee while using her formative experiences of wallowing in teenage crushes and romantic movies to create love stories of her own. The fact that she is now able to spend her spare time searching the Internet for pictures of handsome guys for research purposes is merely a bonus! Come along and visit her Web site at www.allyblake.com.

Ally also writes for the Harlequin® Romance series!

To beautiful, sunny Brisbane.
The city that gave me my first crush,
first kiss, and first love.

CHAPTER ONE

'MR KELLY?'

Dylan looked up from his corner office desk on the thirtieth floor of Kelly Tower to find his assistant, Eric, practically quivering in the doorway. 'Shoot.'

Eric's voice tremored as he tried to say, 'I... There's... I'm not sure I quite know how to...'

Whistling a breath through the smallest gap between his lips, Dylan pushed back his chair and leant his chin upon steepled fingers. 'Take a breath. Visualise your happy place. Count to ten. Whatever it takes. Just remember that I am a very busy, very important man and get to the point.'

Eric did as he was told, so quickly Dylan thought the kid might hyperventilate. But he managed to say, 'I have to get onto your computer for a sec.'

'Go for your life.' Dylan pushed his chair back to give the guy room.

Eric slid into place, his fingers flying over the keyboard with the speed of a kid born with a laptop attached to his thighs. 'A friend of mine works for an online news mag and he messaged me to say I had to see something. This address ought to give us a direct feed.'

Dylan's cheek twitched. 'Seriously, kid, if you've come in here all a fluster because some blog has footage of me feeding spaghetti and meatballs to that nifty little Olympic diver I met in Luxembourg last week…'

His next words froze on his tongue and he slid his chair back beneath his desk with such speed Eric had to leap out of the way.

The monitor was not in fact showing any footage of him. Or the nifty little Olympian. Or meatballs, for that matter.

Dylan didn't even have the chance to be the slightest bit ashamed of his own self-absorption as the crystal clear digital footage brought his *raison d'être*, the family business he championed day in day out, back to the forefront of his mind with a wallop.

The half-acre forecourt keeping Kelly Tower clear of the maddening CBD crowds that traversed Brisbane's hectic George Street had in its north corner a twenty-foot-high, silver, zigzag sculpture—symbolising the impressive escalation of fortune that securing representation with the Kelly Investment Group ensured.

The sculpture usually stood proud and alone bar a few stray pigeons brave enough to cling to its slick diagonal bars. Today it had been taken over by camera crews and reporters with mini-sound recorders and logo-labelled mikes. That kind of excitement had encouraged a crowd of ten times as many interested onlookers.

No wonder.

From what he could make out through the sudden ache descending upon his head, the excitement in the reporter's voice, and Eric wheezing in the doorway, in some kind of crazy protest a woman had handcuffed herself to the zig. Or was it the zag?

Dylan had nothing against handcuffs per se. They had their place in the zeitgeist of the single man. Just not in the middle of a busy workday, not in front of *his* building, and not when as the head of Media Relations it was his job to make the fact that a crazy person had picked that particular statue to attach her daft self seem less interesting than it certainly was.

The crowd parted, and Eric's friend's camera slipped into the gap, giving Dylan a better look at the ruination of his afternoon.

She was fair skinned, dark-eyed, with dark wavy hair made all the more interesting by the fact she kept having to shake its wind-mussed length out of her face. A floral top cinched and flowed in all the right places, telling tales of the kinds of curves and hollows that could distract a weaker-willed man. Not to mention the white calf-length trousers into which her second-glance-worthy bottom had been poured, or the pair of the most insanely high-heeled hot pink sandals…

And, of course, handcuffs.

'What are we going to do?' Eric said in whispered awe.

Dylan jumped; he and the woman had been having such a moment he'd forgotten his assistant was even there.

The heel of his palm reared up over the mouse, ready to jab the webpage closed, when a sudden gust of breeze blew the woman's hair away from her face and she looked directly into Eric's mate's camera lens.

Dylan's hand went rigid a breath from touchdown leaving him staring into a pair of brown eyes. Bambi eyes, for Pete's sake. Big, beautiful, liquid brown with long, delicate eyelashes that made them appear wounded. Vulnerable. Repentant.

His gut twisted. His teeth clenched. A shaft of heat shot him upright, then filled him with adrenalin. Every masculine instinct reached out to him as the deep-seated urge to protect her clobbered him from the inside out. He felt himself rising from his seat, his wrists straightening as though preparing to slay whoever it was who had put that look in those eyes.

Then she licked her lips, shapely pink lips covering the sexiest kind of overbite, and blinked those big brown eyes. As her gaze shifted left she dropped her chin a fraction and she grinned flirtatiously at the person behind the camera.

The trance splintered like broken glass, ringing in his ears as it dislocated around him.

He swore beneath his breath, regained control over his

mouse hand, closed the damn webpage and gave his usually exceptionally discriminating protective instincts a good mental kick in the pants.

They knew better. Far better.

The only people he sheltered by way of his vociferous guard bore the name of Kelly. The blood of his blood. That was as wide as his circle of trust stretched.

His family *needed* to stick together. Tight together. For, no matter how sincere people might seem to be in courting amity, the downside of being richer than Midas and more recognisable than the prime minister was that they would always be considered Kellys first, everything else second.

He'd learnt that lesson nice and young. No matter how beguiling a woman might be, how well bred, how seemingly genuine, they all wanted something from him—his wealth, his connections, even his name.

Nowadays he only let himself play with those who wanted the heat of his body and nothing more. No history and no hereafter. It was a process that had worked beautifully for him for some time.

The fact that not a single one of the warm bodies had stoked the fire of his protective instincts like the one with the soft brown eyes was something he had neither the time nor inclination to ponder.

Feeling mighty fractious, he was out of the chair and through the door before Eric even realised he was moving.

'Sir!' Eric cried.

Dylan waved a hand over his shoulder, and all but ignored the wave of hellos and bowing and scraping that followed in his wake as he jogged down the hallway towards the elevators.

Eric was puffing, red-faced, and his hands were shaking by the time he caught up. 'Tell me what I can do!'

'Don't go anywhere,' Dylan said as the elevator doors closed so slowly he made a mental note to talk to his brother, Cameron—who, being an engineer, surely knew where to source faster-closing ones. 'And tell your mother you'll be late home. I have the feeling this will be a long day.'

Wynnie's wrists hurt.

That's what comes from not doing a trial run with new handcuffs, you duffer.

Ever the pro, she did her all not to let the discomfort show. She dug her fingernails into her palms, hoping it might take away her focus from the itchiness and scratchiness encircling her wrists. And she smiled at the bank of reporters, each of whom had no idea they were about to become her new best friends in this town.

'What's KInG ever done to you?' a voice from the back called out.

She looked down the barrel of the nearest camera, discreetly spat a clump of windswept hair from her lip gloss, and said, 'They've never once returned my phone calls. Typical, right?'

She rolled her eyes, and a few women in the crowd murmured in appreciation.

She made sure to look each and every one of them in the eye as she said, 'The past week I've met with top men and women in local and state government to talk about what we can all do together to help reduce the impact each individual person in this city is having on our environment. Those civil servants, good people with families at home and middle-income jobs, have been full of beans and ideas and enthusiasm. Yet the Kelly Investment Group, the largest company in town, a company with hundreds of employees and capital to burn, has time and again refused to even sit down with me, a new girl in town looking to make new friends, and have a chat over a cuppa.'

More twittering, this time with more volume.

'What does a company have to do to get a cuppa with a girl like you?' a deep voice called out from the back.

Wynnie bit her lip to stop from laughing as that question had come from her one plant at the event—Hannah, her close friend, and fellow Clean Footprint Coalition employee—who was currently hiding behind a cup of takeaway coffee and staring at a radio reporter as though he were the one who'd asked.

Wynnie waited until the crowd quieted. She leant forward, or as far as she could with her hands anchored behind her. 'Kids, today I'm gonna need you all to tap into your imaginations. Hark back to those powerful images of environmentalists in the eighties chaining themselves to bulldozers to stop them knocking down ecologically imperative forests. Fast-forward to the twenty-first century and the corporate giants, such as the Kelly Investment Group—'

Better to use their whole name, she thought, *rather than the cute moniker they'd picked up, or possibly even coined themselves.*

'—are the new bad guys. Collectives with power, and resources, and influence who choose to turn the other cheek while you and I do our bit. We take shorter showers to conserve water, we recycle our newspapers, we unplug our appliances when we're not using them. Right?'

Smiles all around. Lots of nods. If someone held a fist in the air she wouldn't be surprised. The wave of solidarity gripped her. Her heart thundered all the harder in her chest, her skin hummed, the ache in her wrists all but forgotten.

'Did you know,' she said, lowering her voice so they all had to move in closer, 'this sculpture is lit twenty-four hours a day? Yep. Even now, in the middle of a sunny Brisbane spring afternoon, it has thirty separate lights making sure it always looks as shiny as it can possibly be. Thirty!'

One by one the faces turned to glare at the shimmering silver edifice behind her. She could smell blood in the air. That was a triumph in itself considering the Goliath she was putting herself up against.

Her bosses had done their research, looking at popular fashion stores, television stations, national café chains when deciding who to lobby. But every lead had led back to the same destination. The Kellys.

They were the most famous, respected, fascinating family in town. Their reach was unmatched. Their influence priceless. If she got them on board as the first major corporate partner with the revamped Clean Footprint Coalition, the exposure would be unimaginable, and Brisbane would fall into her lap like a pack of cards.

'I am a concerned citizen,' she continued, 'as are you all, as are my colleagues, the band of environmental groups together known as the Clean Footprint Coalition. While the Kelly Investment Group, with the hundreds of ambivalent corporate clients they represent, is the biggest bulldozer you have ever seen.'

Hannah yelled out a mighty, 'Yeah,' and the crowd took up the cry until it all but reverberated around the square.

Wynnie bit back a grin of victory. God, did she love her work. These moments, when she had something to do with making people think about their place in the grand scheme of things, she really felt as if she could change the world.

The rush of pleasure was yummier than chocolate. It was more profound than a Piña Colada on an empty stomach. Hell, it was better than sex. Thank God for that. The hours above and beyond the call of duty that she dedicated to her work were such that she barely remembered what the latter was like.

A sudden ripple of noise from behind her mercifully pulled her from contemplating the extent of her accidental chastity. She turned, as well, and naturally got just far enough that her shoulder jarred, sapping every one of those lovely endorphins with it.

The pain had her sucking in a sharp breath, and hoping the trickle of sweat that had begun its journey down her neck and between her breasts wouldn't show up on camera.

She needn't have worried. Every camera panned left, microphones swerved in their wake, all pointing towards Kelly Tower.

And she knew why her audience had dared stray.

The saucy handcuffs and her subsequent introduction to the media of Brisbane as their new avenging angel had been mere foreplay. For any good show to be newsworthy every angel needed her very own personal devil. And she was about to meet hers.

Little spikes of energy skittered across her skin as she imagined who it might be. An overweight security guard with no authority and less of a clue? Some red-faced lackey sent to try to shoo her away?

'Kelly!' a radio guy called out.

'Mate, over here!' another followed suit.

Kelly? Could one of the gods have come down from the tower himself? She tried to find Hannah's face within the crowd to share the rush. Hannah had her hands on some guy's shoulders as she too tried to make out which bright, shiny Kelly it might be.

As she tried to see without causing a permanent injury Wynnie's mind backtracked over the Kelly family members she'd read about amongst the hundreds of local luminaries she'd been made aware of in the preceding days.

It wouldn't be Quinn Kelly, CEO, surely. The fellow had always been elusive to the mere masses, and of late had become as reclusive as Elvis. She was kind of glad. His ability to slay even the most steely backed opponent with a single glance was legendary.

Brendan Kelly? He was next in charge, the heir to KInG's throne, but not at all press-friendly from what she'd heard. If it was either of them she'd eat her shoes. Mmm. She liked her shoes. They were one of the only things she'd brought with her from Verona. Maybe she'd eat Brussels sprouts. She hated Brussel sprouts so that seemed a fair compromise.

So if it wasn't Quinn, and it wasn't Brendan, and since neither the younger brother Cameron, the engineer, or youngest sister, Meg, the seemingly professional ingénue, worked for KInG, then it had to be the one whose photo she had pulled from the file and stuck to the back of her office door with a great red pin through his forehead. The one she hoped she might *finally* get to after weeks of negotiating, pushing, prodding, making a nuisance of herself. The one she believed could help her make the Clean Footprint Coalition's dream a reality.

Dylan Kelly. Vice President, Media Relations. The spare to Brendan as heir. The public face of KInG, he could charm the heck out of any female with her own televisions, was constantly photographed wining and dining the city's most gorgeous women at benefits, sports events, and everywhere in between, and generally held the gossip-hungry city in thrall.

Wynnie was sure it helped that he appeared to be one of the more beautiful men ever to grace the planet. Her chin had practically hit the conference table when she'd first seen his photo. Heck, if he weren't a corporate bad guy she might have worked pro bono to have him declared a protected species.

'Ladies,' a deep voice rumbled from somewhere over her now throbbing right shoulder. 'Gentlemen. What a pleasure it is to see that you've all decided to come by on this fine sunny day. If I'd have known there was to be a party I would have ordered dim sum and wine coolers for all.'

A few cracks of laughter, several deeply feminine sighs, and the slow flopping of microphones told Wynnie she was losing her audience fast.

She took a deep breath, flicked her hair from her face, and prepared to win them back by beating Mr Slick to an ethical pulp. He might be infamously charming, but she had right on her side, and that had to count for something.

Finally the crowd cleared, and through the parted waters came a man. Standard light blue shirt. Discreetly striped tie. Dark suit. So far not so much the kind of devil she had in mind.

But the closer he got, the more the details came into focus. His suit was tailored precisely to highlight every hard plane of the kind of body that spoke of restrained power, and made walking through big cities at lunchtime a guilty pleasure. His clenched jaw was so sharp it looked to be chiselled from granite. His dark blond hair was short, but with just enough scruff to make a girl want to run her fingers through it. Tame it. Tame him.

But the thing that trapped her gaze and held it was a pair of hooded blue eyes. With all the other inducements he had on show, there was no other colour they'd dare be.

And it was then that she realised they were trained completely on her. Flat, piercing, bewitching baby blue.

And he wasn't merely looking at her, he was looking into her. As if he was searching for the answer to a question only he knew. Her throat tightened and her mouth felt unnaturally dry, and, whatever the question was, the only answer her mind formed was, 'Yes'.

She tried to stand straighter—her handcuffs bit, jerking her back. She found herself twisted in what suddenly felt like a wholly defenceless position—breasts pressed forward, neck exposed. For the first time since she'd snapped the handcuffs closed she wondered if this had been entirely the right move.

'So what's this all about, then?' he asked, his eyes skimming away from her and out into the crowd.

Someone actually had to point a thumb back her way. She rolled her eyes.

He took a moment before turning and spotting her again, using all the subtlety of a double take. She squared her shoulders, looked him in the eye and raised an eyebrow.

He took two slow steps. To an untrained eye he might have seemed as if he was out for a stroll, to her he was clearly a predator stalking his prey. Either way he was nowhere near as cool as he was making himself out to be.

'Well,' he drawled, 'what have we here?'

With the cameras whirring over his shoulder she found perspective. The man before her might be one hell of a kick start for a sorely undernourished libido, but she had to remember he was the devil—though one with enough influence to make a real difference, and she had every intention of making him renounce his bad ways.

She managed to gather a breezy smile. 'Good afternoon.'

He slid his hands into the pockets of his trousers, drawing his shirt tight across his chest, and drawing her eyes to his zipper region in one clever move. 'How's it going?'

'Peachy,' she said, dragging her eyes north. 'Some weather we're having, don't you think?'

His cheek twitched. And he ambled to a halt—close enough that she could all but feel the choleric steam rising from his broad shoulders, but far enough away that every camera on site had access to his captivating face.

He looked away for a moment, and she let go of a lungful of stale breath. He glanced briefly at her high heels, and she figured he planned to keep out of kicking distance. It was the move of a man who'd been in danger of being castrated before. Her confidence came back in a whoosh.

Until he moved closer still. Close enough she could see the rasp of stubble glinting on his cheeks, a loose thread poking out of one of his shirt buttons, the shadow of impressive muscle along his upper arms.

Her nostrils flared as she sucked in oxygen, and the immediate intense physical reaction stunned the hell out of her.

'You've got yourself quite a crowd here,' he said, loud enough everyone could hear.

The cameras and the desperate hush of a dozen journalists reminded her why that was. She gathered her straying wits, tilted her chin downward, batted her eyelashes for all she was worth and, with a cheery smile said, 'Haven't I just?'

The crowd murmured appreciatively. But that wasn't the thing that made her cheeks feel warm, her belly feel tumbly, and her knees feel as weak as if she'd been standing there for days. That was purely due to the fresh, devilish glint in Dylan Kelly's baby blues.

She stood straighter, accidentally jerking her arms and twinging her shoulder, which created a fresh batch of friction at her itchy wrists. Wynnie sucked in a breath to keep from wincing. She kept it all together admirably, promising herself an extra twenty minutes of meditation on the yoga mat when she got home, as she said, 'The handcuffs brought them out. But it's what I have to say that's keeping them here.'

'And what's that?'

Research and appearances backed up the notion that he wasn't a silly man, but he'd just made a silly move. The first rule in shaping public opinion was never to ask a question you didn't know the answer to.

Buoyed anew, she said, 'Since you asked, not a moment before you graced us with your presence, we all agreed that you have been acting terribly irresponsibly, and that it's time you pulled up your socks.'

Before she had the chance to provide some beautiful sound bites dripping with the kinds of statistics newspapers loved, Dylan Kelly grabbed a hunk of suit leg, lifted it high to show off a jet-black sock and enough tanned, muscular, manly calf to create a tidal wave of trembling through the predominantly female crowd.

Okay, so he wasn't at all silly. He was very, very good. Who knew naked male calf could trump handcuffs?

Dylan took the attention and ran with it, on the face of it focusing back on her, but she knew his words were for everyone else. 'You oughtn't to believe all you read in the glossy pages. I'm not all bad. My mother taught me always to wear clean socks, and the hideous memory of my father trying to teach me about the birds and the bees when I was twelve years old scared the bejesus out of me so much it made me the most…responsible man on the planet.'

He might as well have pulled a concertina row of condoms from his pocket as he said it, for the feminine trembling turned to almost feverish laughter as the lot of them got lost in thoughts

of Dylan's underwear and what it might be like to be the one
with whom he might one day act altogether irresponsibly.

The men in the crowd were no better. She could read them
as easily as if they wore flashing signs on their foreheads.
They wanted to buy him a beer, and live vicariously through
him for as long as he'd let them near.

Unless she pulled a shoe-sale sign and a *Playboy* bunny
from somewhere her hands could still reach she might lose
them all for good. It was time *her* press conference was
brought to a close.

'Mr Kelly,' she said, using her outside voice. 'I concede that
your socks are indeed…up. And since my points have obviously fluttered over your head, perhaps I need to be clearer
about what I want.'

The crowd quieted and Dylan Kelly slowly lowered the leg
of his trousers. Again when he looked at her she felt as if he
were looking deep inside her. Testing her mettle? Hoping the
force of his gaze might make her explode into a pile of ashes?
Or was he after something beyond her comprehension?

The ability to stick one's hands on one's hips was under-
rated. As was the ability to cross one's arms. She could only
stand there, torso thrust in his direction, staring back.

His voice dropped until it was so low it felt vaguely threatening. 'Tell me, then, what it is that you want from me.'

'I want you to take the same duty of care with your business
practices, in the example you set for your employees and
clients with regards to your impact on the environment, as you
do your choice of footwear. I want your company to do its part
and reduce its prodigious impact on the environment.'

He slid his feet shoulder-width apart, his toes pointing
directly at her. 'Honey, I'm not sure what you think we do in
there but we sit at computers and wangle phones. Not so
much rainforest felling as you might believe.'

'You might not be the ones swinging the axes, but, by not
being as green as you can be, you may as well be.'

While he looked as though he was imagining ways in which he might surreptitiously have her removed from the face of the earth, she kept her eyes locked on his and was as earnest as she could be when she said, 'Just hear me out. I promise you'll sleep better at night.'

Dylan's eyes narrowed. For a moment she thought she might have pierced his hard shell, until his exquisitely carved cheek lifted into a smile. 'I sleep just fine.'

And she believed him, to the point of imagining a man splayed out on a king-sized bed, expensive sheets barely covering his naked body as he slept the sleep of the completely satiated. Okay, not *a* man. *This* man. *That* body right now unfairly confined by the convention that city financiers wear suits.

She blinked, and her lashes stuck to her hot cheeks reminding her she'd been standing in the sun for half an hour, strapped to a sharp, uncomfortable, metal statue. 'Come on. What do you say? Don't you want your family name to stand for something great?'

Finally, something she said worked. The chiselled jaw turned to rock. The blue eyes completely lost the roguish glint. His faint aura of exasperation evaporated. And right before her eyes the man grew into his suit.

Debonair and cheeky, he was mouth-watering. Focused and switched on he might, she feared and hoped, be the most exceptional devil this angel was yet to meet.

His blue eyes locked hard and fast onto hers, pinning her to the spot with more power than the manacles binding her hands ever could. Her skin flushed, her heart rate doubled, her stomach clenched and released as though readying her to fight or fly.

His voice was rough, but loud enough for every microphone to pick it up as he said, 'Both KInG and the Kelly family invest millions every year in environmental causes such as renewable energy research and reforestation. More than any other company in this state.'

'That's excellent. Truly. But money isn't everything,' she shot back, holding his gaze, feeling the cameras zoom in tight. 'Action is the marker of a man, and the actions within that building beside us in the last year have added up to the waste of more than forty thousand disposable paper cups a *month,* more water usage than the whole of the suburb I live in, and enough paper waste to fell hectares of old forest. What I want from you is the promise that you are going to become the solution rather than being the problem.'

When the devil in the dark suit didn't come back with an instant response her heart thundered with the thrill of a battle won, with the knowledge that the cameras had their sound bite. And if Dylan Kelly, VP Media Relations, was worth his salt he knew in that moment there was no way that he could just walk away.

'So what do ya say?' she said, bringing her voice back down to a more intimate level, loosening her grip, relaxing her stance and slipping on a warm, friendly and just a little bit flirty smile. 'Invite me in for a coffee and a chat and I'll spend tomorrow bugging someone else.'

She felt the whole forecourt hold its collective breath as they awaited his next move.

When it finally came, Wynnie was again glad of her shackles, uncomfortable as they had become, as this time when those blindingly blue eyes met hers they were filled with such self-possession, such provocation, such blatant reined-in heat her knees all but buckled beneath her.

'You want to come up to my place for coffee?' he asked, his voice like silk and melted dark chocolate and all things decadent and delectable and too slippery to hold on to. 'Now why didn't you just say so in the first place?'

CHAPTER TWO

As though Dylan Kelly had a magic button in the pocket of his trousers, Security arrived at that moment to discreetly move the onlookers away. The city workers and tourists had had their free lunchtime show. The press had their story. Wynnie's awareness campaign was off to a flying start. Everyone was happy.

Everyone except Dylan, who was staring at her as if she were a piece of gum stuck to the bottom of his shoe.

'That was a cheap trick you just pulled,' he growled quietly enough that only she could hear.

Wynnie shook her hair out of her face. Now the crowd had dispersed, the breeze whipping up George Street was swirling around her like a maelstrom. 'I prefer fearless, indomitable and inventive.'

'In the end it will be they who decide one way or the other.' He motioned with a slight tilt of his head to the row of news vans on the sidewalk.

'Lucky for me,' she said with a smile.

'Mmm. Lucky for you.' He glanced at his watch, then back at her. 'So did you want to conduct your bogus meeting out here or were you planning on staying here for the night?'

Wynnie twisted to get her hands to the tight back pocket of her capri pants, which had been ideal for the Verona autumn she had left behind, but in the warm Brisbane spring sunshine they stuck to her like a wetsuit. 'Oh, no. I'm done. Horizontal is my much preferred method. Of sleeping,' she added far too late for comfort.

She glanced up to find him thankfully preoccupied enough to have missed her little Freudian slip. Unfortunately he was preoccupied with the twisting and turning of her hips.

His voice was deep, his jaw tight, when he said, 'I could have had you arrested, you know. This is private property.'

'Nah,' she said. 'The globe belongs to none of us.'

He'd moved closer, having seemingly reconciled himself to the fact that she wanted to get out of the handcuffs as much as he wanted her to, and that her shoes were made for looks and functionality, not for use as a secret weapon. Without the clamour of the crowd making the square smell like a fish-market, she caught a waft of his aftershave—clean, dark, expensive. Suddenly she felt very, very thirsty.

Despite his focus, she twisted some more. Her shoulder twinged but better that than have to keep trying to appear professional while cuffed to the statue, and while the touch of his eyes made her skin scorch beneath her clothes.

Her fingers made it to the bottom of the tight coin pocket to find it was empty. Her heart leapt into her throat until she remembered she'd put the tiny key inside the breast pocket of her shirt at the last minute.

Naturally when she tried to reach it, she couldn't. She stood on tiptoes, looking for Hannah, knowing it was a lost cause. She would have been back at the office the minute lunch hour was up.

Wynnie closed her eyes a moment, took a deep breath and said, 'Would you do me a favour?'

Dylan's deep voice rolled over her. 'You certainly aren't backwards about asking for what you want, I'll give you that.'

'I need you to get the key for my cuffs.'

After a long, slow pause he said, 'The key?'

She squeezed her eyes shut tighter. 'It's in my top right

breast pocket. I can't reach it. So unless you do want me to become a permanent fixture—'

The rest of her words dried up in her throat and her eyes sprang open.

It seemed she hadn't had to ask twice. Dylan's hand was already sliding into the pocket, his fingertips brushing against the soft cotton over her bra; just slowly enough to make a ripple of goose bumps leap up all over her body, and just fast enough she couldn't accuse him of taking advantage.

All too soon he held up the key. 'This the one you're after?'

She hoped to God it was. If he made another foray in there she didn't know what she might do.

She nodded and looked up into his eyes. Up close they were the colour of the sky back home, the unspoilt wilds of country Nimbin—the kind of wide-open blue found only in the most untouched places on earth. But the colour was the only virtuous thing about them. Barely checked exasperation boiled just below the surface.

She lifted her hand to take the key, was reminded why he had it in the first place, then gritted her teeth as she twisted so that she could expose her wrists, and her back view, to him instead.

This time he managed to have her unlocked without touching her at all. Not even a whisper, an accidental grope, a playful pat. She actually felt disappointed.

When God was handing out the mechanism for knowing who a girl could safely lean on, Wynnie had so-o-o missed out. If there was ever a man in her vicinity who was about to act against her own interests, that was the one she was drawn to.

She shook her head and vowed to ask Hannah to set her up on some sort of blind date and fast. Or maybe just a night out dancing at some dark, hazy club. Or she could take up running. Not as though she'd ever lifted a foot in purposeful exercise in her life, but there was no time like the present to begin! If she didn't manage to release some of the sexual tension this man had summoned, she was going to make a hash of everything.

She slid the cuffs from her right wrist, sucking in a short sharp breath as the pain of their release grew worse than the dull ache of the wearing of them.

'Are you okay?' he asked, and she looked up in surprise.

For the briefest moment she thought she saw actual concern flicker within his gaze. She blinked and it was gone. She hid the cuffs and her red wrists behind her. 'I'm fine. Now how about that coffee?'

'First things first,' he said, rocking forwards on his heels until her personal space became his personal space. His dark scent became her oxygen. His natural heat her reason for getting up that morning.

Her toes curled and her tongue darted out to wet her lips.

'I don't make a habit of having coffee with a woman without at the very least getting a name.' He held out a hand. 'Dylan Kelly.'

Wynnie blinked, mentally slapped herself across the back of her head for letting her imagination run rampant, then took his hand, doing her best to ignore the frisson of heat that scooted up her arm as his fingers curled around hers. 'Wynnie Devereaux.'

His eyebrows rose. 'French?'

'Australian.'

His eyebrows slowly flattened out, but the edge of his mouth kicked up into a half smile as he realised she had no intention of illuminating him further.

The truth was that Devereaux was the maiden name of a grandmother she'd never met, and her little brother, Felix, had never been able to pronounce her real name as a baby and had called her Wynnie from the time he could talk.

Felix. The whisper of his name in the back of her mind made her soul hurt, and reminded her how her patchy instinct on who to trust could go so terribly wrong.

Either way, she had no intention of talking to Dylan Kelly, or anyone else, about the existence of her brother. Or, for that matter, her real name.

'Next,' he said. *Before I inflict you upon my place of business*, he didn't need to say. 'Are you here on your own whim or as an ambassador for others like you?'

Wynnie raised an eyebrow at his snarky attitude. She then pulled a business card from the skinny travel purse looped beneath her shirt and hanging against her hip.

Her fingers brushed over the crystal and white-stone butterfly clip attached to the strap of her purse, and like the touchstone it was, it helped take the edge off her soaring adrenalin.

She handed her card over, a handcuff still dangling from that wrist.

The whisper of a half-smile tugged at Dylan's mouth, and her body reacted the same way it had every time that happened. It stretched and unfolded and purred.

Which was insane. He'd made no bones about how unenthusiastic he was about the prospect of spending time with her. And he was a target, not some anonymous hot guy in a club who might, if she was very lucky, turn out to be an undemanding friend with benefits. But she couldn't help herself. It was as though the laws of nature were having their way with her without her consent.

She whipped the cuffs behind her and unhooked them, shoving one end down the back of her trousers before they became more of a distraction. Or an apparent invitation.

He glanced at her for one long moment more before his eyes slid to her business card. His lip curled as he said, 'You're a *lobbyist*?'

'Is that better or worse than whatever it was you were thinking I was before you saw the card?'

He tipped her business card into the palm of his hand and out of sight. And if she'd thought he'd filled out his suit before, now he stood so erect he looked as if he'd been sewn into the thing. 'To tell you the truth,' he said, 'I'm not sure.'

But at least he waved an arm in front of her, herding her towards the formidable Kelly Tower.

As Wynnie's feet moved under her she realised she was kind of stunned. The spectacle had actually worked. Her employers, whose previous public persona was devout and dull, would come out of this appearing anything but. They would get prime-time news coverage, and she had gathered several leads with reporters who wanted follow-ups. She couldn't have asked for more.

The fact that she was now heading inside enemy camp meant she was a few steps ahead of the game.

So naturally she had none of the meticulously prepared, Kelly-centric pamphlets loaded with detailed cost projections and time frames on hand to back her up. There was no room in her purse for more than a credit card and house key. And nothing else was going to fit down those trousers.

Well, she'd be fine. She'd just have to wing it. Having grown up with hippy parents in Nimbin, the flower-child capital of Australia, spouting green was what she had been born to do.

She snuck a glance sideways at her silent new acquaintance to find his profile was even more daunting than front-on. His thick, dark blond hair was being lightly and sexily ruffled by the breeze shooting around the building. Those stunning blue eyes were hooded beneath strong brows so that they looked to be peering down at the world via his perfectly carved nose. And then there were those lips.

She wondered which lucky girl out there was allowed to kiss them whenever she pleased. Was able to run her finger across their planes whenever the fancy took her. Was able to lean her chin on her palm and watch them as they talked, and smiled and laughed. Her own lips tingled just looking at them.

His cheek dimpled and she knew she'd been caught staring. As he turned his head her chin shot skyward so that she might pretend to be taken with the facade of the skyscraper named after his equally daunting family.

She lifted her right hand to shield her eyes from the glare

shooting off the glass panels of the top floors when pain bit her shoulder. She crumpled in on herself and let out a shocked squeal.

He noticed. This time there was no mistaking the flicker of a supporting arm in her direction. 'Are you *sure* you're okay?'

She grabbed the handle of a glass door leading inside, using her left hand. 'Once you're standing beside me in front of a bank of cameras, telling the people of Brisbane the ways in which you and your company have helped reduce your impact on the planet thanks to the help of the Clean Footprint Coalition, and admitting how easy it will be for every individual sitting there on their couch at home to follow suit, then I'll be ecstatic. Until then, assume I'm about middling.'

She pulled open the door and, with her head held high, stalked through.

The thick glass wasn't thick enough to shield her from the surge of laughter tumbling from Dylan's beautiful lips. Or the ripple of awareness that lathered her entire body at the seriously sexy sound.

She frowned. He didn't need to be declared a protected species. He needed a warning label stapled to his head. *Beware: come within ten feet and your sexual appetite will exceed local limits.*

A few more steps inside and Wynnie's high heels clacked noisily to a halt as she tipped her head back, spun about and assimilated the Kelly Tower's entryway.

Acres of golden marble floors were only made more stunning by the most intricate black marble inlays. Two-storey-high columns acting as sentinels to a long hallway leading away from the front doors were lit by reproduction antique gas lamps. Numerous arched windows a floor above let in streams of natural light. And a massive clock, twice her height, ticked away the minutes until the banking day was closed.

It was the most stunning space she had ever seen. And that was just the lobby.

The CFC think tank had been spot on. This place, this *family* were the right choice. If the businesses of Brisbane didn't all secretly want to be them, if every single citizen didn't want to do behind closed doors exactly as they did, then she might as well have stayed in Verona.

That would have kept her from spending the past glorious month hanging with Hannah, her closest friend in the whole world. It would have kept her from working for an organisation that rang her bells like no other on earth. It would have kept her tens of thousands of miles from the beautiful place she grew up rather than a few hours' drive...

'You can buy a postcard with this exact view from the newsstand on the corner,' a deep voice rumbled from just behind her.

She turned to him, her legs twisted awkwardly and a hunk of hair caught in her eyelashes. As elegantly as humanly possible she disentangled herself. 'Not necessary.'

'Then would you care to accompany me upstairs?' he asked.

Right. Yes. She might be inside his lair but the hard work had barely begun.

It was game on. His job was easy—all he had to say was 'no', over and over again. Hers was nearby impossible—all she had to do was get him to say 'yes'.

She took a deep breath and followed Dylan into the large art-deco lift. Going with the catch-more-flies-with-honey theory of negotiation, she cocked a hip and smiled at his reflection. 'Why do I get the feeling I'm not the first girl you've invited into your office for coffee?'

Though the rest of him could have been cut from the same marble as that in the lobby, a flicker of heat ignited in his eyes. They were his tell. The one sign that she had that maybe one day his 'no' might turn into a 'yes'. Lucky for her, looking into them was no chore.

As long as she gave no tell of her own. She didn't need him knowing that her need to get this job done right was as impor-

tant to her as anything she'd ever done. Or that her body was
as attuned to his as a weathercock channelling a coming storm.

Dylan took a seat behind his one of a kind, polished-oak desk,
and waited for Eric to lay out a chai latte for his unexpected
two-o'clock appointment and a sweet black for him. He unbuttoned his cuffs and rolled up his sleeves in preparation for
whatever the hell else would be thrown at him this afternoon.

Eric moved to the doorway, half terrified and half smitten
with the creature ambling about the office. His eyes begged
Dylan to let him back in. But this was one meeting he was
doing all on his lonesome. Dylan shook his head once and the
door closed with a pathetic click.

'What happened to Jerry?' Dylan asked as he waved a
hand at the couch on the opposite side of his desk.

Wynnie remained standing as she picked up her mug and
blew cool air across the top. 'Jerry who?'

He tried dragging his eyes away from the small round hole
formed between her full lips, but then realised he might as
well get his enjoyment from this unfortunate meeting where
he could. 'Your predecessor at the CFC.'

'Oh. He doesn't work there anymore, and now I do.'

Dylan's cheek twitched, and not for the first time that day.

Meeting Wynnie Devereaux in the flesh had done nothing
to temper the fact that at first glance she'd seemed just the kind
of woman he would normally like to sink his teeth into after
a long day at work—pocket-sized, hot-blooded, skin like
fresh cream.

Half an hour in her presence had told him she was also just
about the most infuriating creature he'd ever met. She was a
lobbyist, of all the rotten things—a professional charmer
who'd chosen his family to lure to her cause. She *had* to be
new in town or she would have known better than to come
gunning for him.

Still, for one tiny moment out there in the forecourt, something in those absorbing brown eyes had yet again charmed him. And as that chink in his usually rock-hard armour lay exposed she'd been able to confound him, twist his words and finally outfox him at his own game. All that with both hands strapped behind her back.

His gaze meandered away from her lips to her small hands. Both of her wrists were so pink and painfully chaffed that his own itched and stung in empathy. And the instinct to soothe the hurt, to make it his own, slammed him from nowhere once more. Only this time he managed to catch himself in time before, like a sucker, he asked her if she was okay.

He shifted on his seat. Every part of him uncomfortable, some for different reasons than others. 'If you're hoping to find where I keep the busts of the baby seal cubs I club for fun, they're in my home office.'

Her mouth curved into a smile. 'Right by the barrels of crude oil you spill into the river at night just for kicks.'

'You have done your research. So, where were you before the CFC?'

That had her eyes sliding back to his. Despite himself he searched their depths for the singular vulnerability that kept grabbing him through the middle. Now all he saw was the rush and fire of fierce intelligence. Unfortunately it didn't serve to squash the attraction nipping at his skin.

She said, 'Where I've come from is not important.'

'It is if you wish to finish that coffee before my burly security guards throw you out on your sweet backside.'

She gave him a blank stare, but she couldn't hide the rise and fall of her throat as she swallowed. She slowly took her seat, put her half-drunk chai latte on the edge of his desk, crossed her legs and dug in.

He hid his smile as he pretended to look for something in the top drawer of his desk. Poor old Jerry would have been quivering by now. And apologising. And practically offering to throw *himself* out.

Then again, he would never have accused Jerry of having a sweet backside. True, Jerry had never managed to be alone in a room with him before and he hadn't been as close to Jerry's backside as he had to Wynnie Devereaux's...

The few remaining bits of him that weren't coiled like springs coiled now, so tight they ached as he relived her turning her sweet backside his way so that he could set her free of her restraints.

Curves poured into tight white fabric, thick but not completely opaque, offering him the faint outline of a floral G-string. A flash of creamy skin peeking out from between her beltline and her shirt. His hand following the gentle curve but not touching. How did he manage to get so close without touching...?

Who was he kidding? The painful pleasure of those few moments of deliberate self-restraint were the highlight of his week.

He shut his drawer, sat back in his chair. Now he *really* wanted to know where the CFC had found her. And he made a mental note to get HR to headhunt their headhunter.

Her nostrils flared as she took in a breath. 'Mr Kelly, what I've done before is not nearly as important as why I am here. My method of getting the name Clean Footprint Coalition on everyone's lips may not have been typical by any means, but my mission is a deadly serious one. The CFC is a collective of respectable, hopeful, forward-thinking people. And it's clear to all of us that KInG needs to go green, and quick smart.'

She sat forward, shuffled her sweet backside to the very edge of her chair and gripped the perimeter of his desk.

'I need you,' she said.

Her breathy voice came to him on a plea. A vulnerable, naked, genuine supplication. His own ability to breathe seemed to have gone walkabout as all the blood in his body was suddenly needed elsewhere.

She was good. More than good. She was a siren with a mission. But then, right when she had him where surely she wanted him, she seemed to recognise exactly how she had affected him, and her fingers uncurled from the edge of his desk and she sat slowly back in her chair. Confounding woman.

'Our organisation,' she said with added emphasis, 'needs KInG. And KInG need us. Getting into bed together is win-win for all of us.'

He shifted on his seat again, knowing he was running out of positions in which he could sit upright and not hurt himself. At least he saw a chance to give her a taste of her own medicine.

'All of us, hey?' he said. 'For some reason I'm seeing futons involved and that's just not my style.'

She shook her head, and seemed to struggle to find her words, the siren lost within the skin of a delightfully befuddled mortal woman. 'Forget getting into bed.'

'But now you've brought it up, it's out there. I like big beds, not too firm, with plenty of room to move.'

She held out a steadying hand, as if willing him with every fibre of her being to shut up and let her finish. 'I meant it's a win-win situation for both companies. We are looking to make a difference, and just think of all the lovely, happy, warm, free PR that would come to KInG if you led the way on how to be an authentically green business.'

An electronic Post-it note blinked up onto Dylan's computer from Eric, telling him he had a client waiting. 'You have two more minutes. Give it to me straight up. What exactly do you want?'

'A partnership.'

Dylan couldn't help himself, he laughed. Her responding dark frown was adorable.

'With KInG?' he clarified.

'And the Clean Footprint Coalition.'

He leant forward. 'Honey, I'm not sure which hay cart you rolled in on, but somebody's been pulling your leg if they gave you any indication that this company had any desire, need or care to be in cahoots with anyone.'

She leant in towards him, too, recrossing her legs, and giving eye contact as good as she got. 'But you already are. Your largest corporate clients are in car manufacturing, oil production, shipping, some of the largest polluters on the planet. Is that something you'd rather we were focusing on in our press material?'

The skin beneath his left eye twitched. It was a timely reminder that no matter how adorable her frowns might be she had an agenda, and it involved targeting his family in her tree-hugging games. If she backed him any further into a corner he would have no choice but to claw his way back out, and if she was in his way so be it.

His voice was as sharp as cut glass as he asked, 'So why the hell didn't you chain yourself to a sculpture outside one of their businesses?'

Rather than sensing how close she was to grave danger, the minx smiled, her eyes gleaming like warm honey. 'I like yours better.'

Dylan growled. He actually growled, right out loud, and shook his fists beneath his desk. And right when his frustration reached its peak, her voice came to him like hot chocolate on a cold night. 'Mr Kelly, I told you a small fib when I promised to bother someone else tomorrow. You're it; the only company I even have on my radar. My every working hour has been and will be focused on bringing you home. So why not save us both some time, and a lot of aggravation and let my people come in here, strip you down to your bare essentials and build you back up again when it comes to energy consumption, consumables and waste? You'll barely notice the cost and you will go to bed knowing the planet is breathing better for your minimal efforts.'

'Why me?' he asked, questioning not only her but whichever god he'd annoyed enough that day to bring this woman to his doorstep.

'You are the company every other one in the country wants to emulate. Your success is legendary. Your influence off the chart. Where you lead others will follow, and we want them to follow. Turn off one light overnight, who'd notice? Turn off all the lights of Brisbane overnight, and it's a revolution.'

She took a breath, licked her lips, sent his body temperature up a notch in the process, then said, 'So what do you think?'

He leant back in his chair, but his eyes never once left hers. 'Here it is, hopefully clear enough none of it will flutter over *your* head. I do not respond well to threats. I do not respond well to having my business or my family singled out so publicly by upstarts with an agenda. I think the stunt you pulled out there might be a lucky winner for one news cycle, but in taking me on you have bitten off more than you can chew. I think you should shine your green light elsewhere before you find it's dimmed forever.'

She blinked up at him, those warm brown eyes somehow holding in whatever it was that *she* was thinking. Eventually she uncrossed her legs and she stood. She ran her hands down the sides of her thighs and he noticed they were shaking. His gut clenched. He pinched himself on the arm, hard.

She gave a small nod, and said, 'Okay, then. That sounds like my cue to thank you for your time and let you get on with your day.'

She made her way to the door of his office. He pushed himself from his chair and followed. Halfway there he laid a hand on her lower back to guide her. Guide her? It was a straight line to the office door. He held his hand as still as could be while the muscles of her back and hips slid against him in an erotic rhythm.

There was no professional reason to touch her. If she'd been Jerry he wouldn't have even left his chair. If she'd been Jerry she wouldn't have made it past the front door. He was touching her as a lightning rod, as a way to stop himself from doing anything more extreme.

When she reached the hallway and turned towards him, his hand slid around her waist. The twist of her shirt, the soft dip of warm skin… He pulled his hand away quick smart.

She looked at him as though she had no clue as to the commotion raging inside him. 'Thank you,' she said, 'for this afternoon. We appreciate your time.'

Suddenly he found himself not quite ready to have seen the last of her. He leant his shoulder against the doorframe of his office door. 'Thank *you* for this afternoon. It has to be the most eventful Tuesday we've seen around this place since Melbourne Cup Day.'

'Stock prices soar by triple figures, did they?'

His laughter carried out into the hall and several lackeys rushing past stopped to see why. He ignored them and explained, 'A bunch of guys and girls from the legal floor dressed up as horses and jockeys and replayed the race for our amusement.'

She raised an eyebrow. 'Well, I can only hope that when you tell the board about our meeting today you do so with as much verve and enthusiasm as you had for an inter-office lark.'

Her voice was pure sarcasm, yet she stayed where she was on the ocean of polished wood with its discreetly papered walls and sculpted cornices, and flurry of assistants keeping the place abuzz, and she clung to her small purse with both hands.

And it hit him like a three-foot fishhook through the guts. She wanted more than their two companies to work together. She wanted him. She was standing there acting as if she had ants in her pants as she was crushing on him big-time.

For the briefest moment he imagined sliding a hand into the back of her hair, pulling her to him and kissing the daylights out of her.

It rankled. He wasn't the kind of guy to get suckered in by the simple sweet tug of desire. Only those of a particularly cool and indifferent ilk warranted his time. And Wynnie Devereaux appeared neither cool nor indifferent. While she was outwardly vivacious and implacable, he had the sense that on the inside she was as fragile and beautiful as the jewelled butterfly her fingers were tracing on her purse.

She was also a lobbyist working the other side of the table.

He pushed his way back upright and looked into her eyes just long enough that he didn't feel the strange, warm, encouraging trap closing over him, and said, 'I'll plant a tree this weekend and think of you.'

Her full lips curved into a slow smile. 'Plant a dozen and think of your kids.'

'I don't have kids.' He added a wink. 'So far as I know. Goodbye, Wynnie.'

'Till next time, Mr Kelly.'

After one last long look, one he understood all too well, she turned and walked down the hallway.

He couldn't help but grin when he spotted one half of her handcuffs swaying and bouncing against her sweet backside until she rounded the corner, out of sight.

CHAPTER THREE

WYNNIE nudged her high heels off her feet, let them fall to the floor beneath her bar stool, and massaged one bare foot with the other. She then closed her eyes and pressed her fingers into the tops of her eyelids.

'What are you doing?' Hannah asked.

'Trying to permanently block out several particular moments of my day.'

Hannah laughed. 'Come off it. You did brilliantly! Better than we could ever have hoped. You've already made the four-thirty reports. You actually got inside the building. As far as the CFC is concerned you're a rainmaker.'

'Nevertheless I'm still of the opinion that threatening to start a campaign whereby I would blame the most influential business in town with single-handedly poisoning the planet on purpose was a real high point.'

Wynnie let her head thunk onto the shiny red bar of the funky Eagle St Pier beer garden. But the knock to the head did nothing to shift the images stuck fast to the outer curve of her skull.

Dylan Kelly's knee-weakening half-smiles when she flirted with him. His debilitating dark smiles when she pushed him a step too far. And most of all his delicious parting smile, which had made her think, for one brief shining moment, that maybe she wasn't the only one who'd spent the afternoon having a professional conversation on the outside and a very personal one on the inside.

'Nah,' Hannah said before downing the rest of her cocktail in one gulp and asking for another in one swift move. 'I'm going to have to vote for the nickel allergy as my favourite Wynnie moment.'

Wynnie lifted her head, flicked her fringe away from her face and ran gentle fingers over the bandages on her wrists. 'That's not funny.'

Hannah laughed so loud a dozen heads turned to see what they were missing. 'Right. You went from making a business contact no one at the CFC has ever managed to wangle, to having a just-out-of-med-school doctor diagnose you with being too cheap to buy quality handcuffs.'

Wynnie sat on her hands. 'No way was I going to use the funds of a non-profit organisation to spend as much as I could on top-of-the-line handcuffs.'

Hannah only laughed so hard she had to push her stool back so that she could clutch her stomach. Wynnie grabbed her so-called friend by the belt loops of her jeans and tugged her upright before she took out some passer-by.

As Hannah continued to giggle Wynnie took a deep breath, drinking in the aroma of beer and lemon-scented banksias filling big earthenware pots around the floor. It was a deeply Australian smell, and, after many years living abroad, it was unexpectedly comforting. As were the last vestiges of Brisbane spring sunshine pouring through massive skylights and floor-to-ceiling windows.

The labours of her day finally began to ease away.

Wynnie glanced down the bar. 'I'm not sure if a nickel overdose can make a person thirsty but I am dying for another drink.'

Problem was, since she was on cortisone for her red wrists, she had to stick with pineapple juice, which did nothing to help her forget Dylan Kelly's brawny forearms, the curve of short thick hair that turned from gold to brown just above his ears and those deep, glinting, hooded blue eyes.

When their drinks arrived, the nice barman had added a sugared strawberry to the edge of her glass, and an umbrella for good measure. He also gave her a long smile.

He was terribly cute. She was pathologically single. And obviously in need of some mollifying male company if her performance that afternoon was anything to go by.

But there was a kind of puppy-dog softness about the eyes that told her he was a boyfriend kind of guy. Girlfriends shared stories of family and past folly as pillow talk, something she'd never be able to do, which meant she'd never be a girlfriend kind of girl.

She gave him a short nod, then turned her body away from the bar and towards Hannah, who was grinning at her over her Fuzzy Navel.

'Wynnie has a new little friend,' Hannah sing-songed.

'Wynnie has no such thing.'

'Give him another five minutes and he'll be back with a rose between his teeth and a mandolin. Better yet, you order the next round of drinks and save us twenty bucks.'

'Don't be ridiculous.'

'And why not? A new man for a new town. After the hours you've put in this month you deserve to let your hair down some.'

Wynnie raised a hand to her hair, which she'd pinned up off her neck while at the doctor's surgery, sliding her butterfly clip above her ear to hold back her fringe. 'It was down today. And look where that got me.'

'Ah,' Hannah said, with way too much of an inflection.

'What does "ah" mean?'

'It means so that's why you're all down about the mouth when considering the success your day has been you should be as high as a kite.'

'I'm not high because I'm not the one on my fourth cocktail,' she said out of the side of her mouth.

Hannah waggled a wobbly finger in her general direction. 'First my little recruit has proven herself professionally, making me look shiny and fabulous for insisting she be hired, and now she has gone and got herself a little crush on Mr Dylan Tall Blond and Handsome Kelly. I'm celebrating!'

Wynnie's naked feet pointed hard at the floor as some kind of strange physical response shot through her at the mere mention of Dylan Kelly's name.

She opened her mouth wide to deny everything, but suddenly she was too exhausted to bother. 'It might have been nice to have a heads up that he is that gorgeous.'

'I thought the fact that I had to wipe drool from my chin every time his name was mentioned in passing during strategy meetings was giveaway enough.'

'Not nearly enough. You do know he's stunning. Matinee-idol, suit-model, high-school-crush, knee-weakening, super-models-only-need-apply stunning.'

'Did your voice just crack a little?'

'It did not,' Wynnie shot back. Then for some unknown reason added, 'But it's not just his looks. He's sharp, and focused, and canny and funny when you don't expect it.'

'So I've heard. But I am a respected lawyer, you know. I must show some decorum. Did you? Show decorum?'

Wynnie's hands went straight to her eyes to rub them again. 'I might have become a tad tongue-tied on more than one occasion, and made inferences that I wanted to go to bed with him, but that's it.'

Hannah's laughter turned heads the whole way around the bar. 'So are you gonna ask him out or not?'

Her hot hands dropped to cup her blissfully cold glass. 'For what purpose?'

'Um, dinner, a movie, the horizontal tango?'

'Han! He's *the* only mark. The one who can make or break this deal.'

'And that's why you won't ask him out?'

'No. Yes! Well, that and the fact that he's probably got a line-up of women wiping drool from their chins.'

Hannah's answering smile was most unfriendly.

'My working hours are far too full on right now to even think about starting up any kind of anything with any man.'

'Anything else?'

'Yeah, he's just a huge flirt. He flirted with me, every female reporter within eyeshot, some of the men, and a pot plant on the way into his office. It's pathological.'

'Finally something I understand! Now this isn't the kind of thing you would have found in the stuff the researchers gave you, so here goes. The stories do circulate that he is… How do I put this?' Hannah tapped her chin and looked to the heavens. 'He's a man with a limited attention span.'

'Meaning?'

'Never appears to date the same girl twice. Though they are all beautiful. All fabulous. All about as warm as ice sculptures.'

Wynnie blinked. 'And you think I might be interested in being one of those girls of the week, and that I fit that description? I'm not sure which part of that I should be insulted by most.'

Hannah slapped her on the arm. 'Stop trying to be offended and think about it. You've found time this month to come bowling with me, to go out for drinks, to see a movie, a bunch of DVDs. I could sacrifice a little of that down time for the sake of your love life before you start sleeping in the office to get a head start on the working day and unknowingly muttering carbon emission averages beneath your breath.'

Wynnie shook her head. 'It feels like things have fallen into place for me for the first time in a really long time. I *believe* in the organisation with every fibre of my being. Their philosophy is my very lifeblood. To be their advocate is an honour and an obligation. Every hour I spend working for them I feel like I am contributing, and helping and redeeming…'

She shook her head hard and let her voice drift away.

Of all the people she could have talked to about her acute need to make amends, Hannah was it. She'd been with Wynnie the day Felix had disappeared—even finding her a great lawyer through her professors at school. But even after all this time, saying the words out loud felt too raw.

'I'm not asking Dylan Kelly out. Okay?'

She sipped at her drink. All of the excuses were fine but they didn't come close to her main reticence. She'd been known to do stunningly self-sacrificing things for men she regarded highly, and the only way to never let that happen again was not to put herself in the position where it might.

There were only so many times a girl could change her hair, and her name, and leave town. In comparison, putting up with a little sexual tension was small fry.

Hannah leant her elbow on the bar and her head on her hand. 'You done?'

She nodded.

'So you wouldn't mind, then, if Dylan Kelly and I became hot and heavy.'

Wynnie gripped the straw between her teeth. 'Not in the least,' she fibbed.

'What about me and the bartender?'

Wynnie all but bounced on her bar stool. 'Oh, do! He seems nice and sweet, the ideal complement to your rabid cynicism. And he could make you cocktails every night. He's perfect for you!'

Wynnie's bottom bouncing came to a halt when she realised Hannah had been pulling her leg about the bartender to get a true answer about Lady Killer Kelly. And she'd given it in surround sound, with Technicolor and subtitles.

'I have to go,' Wynnie said, finding her shoes with her feet. 'The local farmer's market closes at eight and I'm all out of kumquats.'

She grabbed her battered travel purse from the bar, slid her feet back into her shoes, hopped off the bar stool and pressed her way through the crowd.

'Kumquats? That's one I've never heard before.' Hannah, three inches taller than Wynnie even in her flats, caught up all too easily. 'And just because you thought the sun shone from Felix's you-know-what and he turned out to be a total screw-up that doesn't mean every man you ever meet will do the same. Trust me.'

Wynnie saw a gap open up within a huge group of uni students and took it. Alone.

A screw-up? Felix hadn't just been a screw-up. Her kid brother, her only remaining family, the beautiful boy who'd never even had the heart to step on a spider he was so attuned with the world around him, had done something so heinous, so out of character, hurting people all in the name of saving the planet. And to add insult to injury he'd left *her* to clean up the mess she hadn't even seen coming. And she'd never laid eyes on him since.

Trust was now a four-letter word.

When she reached the sidewalk she bounced on her toes as her eyes scanned the streets for an empty taxi.

'Heard from him yet?' Hannah asked from beside her.

There was no point pretending she didn't know Hannah was talking about her brother. She shook her head so hard her butterfly came loose. She reached out and caught it before it hit the ground. Her heart thundered in her ears at the thought she might have broken it—the only thing she still had that had once belonged to her beautiful, brilliant, progressive parents. She could only be thankful they had both gone by the time Felix changed.

'You will, sweetie,' Hannah said. 'Don't worry. He always

checks in eventually. Though why he doesn't just leave you the hell alone once and for all I have no idea.'

She glared at Hannah, who held up her hands in surrender.

'Fine. I won't say another word on the subject. But if I ever bump into him in a dark alley all he's getting from me is a swift kick up the backside.'

A taxi stopped. Wynnie put her butterfly into her purse and opened the back door. She took a breath and turned to her friend. 'Is that your version of not another word?'

'From this moment on, I cross my heart.' Then she looked back inside the bar. 'A cute bartender who can give me free drinks, or the infamous Dylan Kelly who can buy me the bar. Mmm, how is a girl to choose?'

Wynnie poked out her tongue and jumped in the cab, giving the driver the address of the Spring Hill cottage the CFC had put her up in as part of her irresistible relocation package.

After watching through the back window to see Hannah grab the next taxi that came along, Wynnie leant into the hot fabric seat, let out a long, slow breath and closed her eyes.

Only to be confronted with Dylan Kelly in full colour and three dimensions. This time instead of trying to squeeze him from her brain she let him simmer there a while.

Her breast ached where his fingers had brushed her. Her backside ached where they hadn't. She wished her wrists still hurt and then she might not have noticed the rest, but magical white cream was keeping the most sensible of her itches at bay.

Who was she kidding? They were on two different planes of existence. The audacious, hippy environmentalist and the formidable, filthy-rich corporate giant.

And really, when it came down to it, thank goodness for that.

Dylan sat back from the dinner table, replete. Another rambunctious Kelly family dinner done with.

The minute he'd hit the long table in his parents' over-decorated dining hall, he'd eaten like a man possessed.

Caramelised pork with green papaya salad, duck breast with blood orange & quince marmalade, goat's cheese baklava. He'd not missed an offering, filling his stomach in an effort to quell that other hunger that had cloaked him all afternoon.

Wynnie Devereaux might have been a pain in his behind, but she'd also left him with an ache everywhere else. He'd felt her liquid brown eyes grazing his cheek all afternoon until he'd taken to his office washroom and shaved. His palm had tingled with the feel of her hip sliding against it until he'd purposely scalded himself on a too-hot cup of coffee. No matter the hundred other jobs he'd had to do, he hadn't been able to erase her from his mind.

It certainly hadn't helped that his phone had run hot all afternoon from media outlets looking for quotable quotes about his relationship with the CFC and his opinion on the woman of the hour.

Having to find new and interesting ways of *not* saying he mostly wanted to throw her over his shoulder and give her a good spank had taken its toll.

Food and lots of it had worked for a couple of hours which had made for a nice relief. As had making mention of the incident, every chance he'd had. He patted his tight belly. So long as he didn't make fuelling his sexual appetite with food a habit.

'Are you sure you're done there, bro?' his younger sister, Meg, asked. 'For five bucks I'll let you lick my plate.'

He offered her a shark's grin. 'The day you put in an honest day's work at an honest job, then you'll understand why some of us need big dinners. We often miss lunch rather than make it the focus of our day.'

She poked out her tongue and took off into the next room with her mobile phone already glued to her ear.

'She's almost thirty, right?' he asked his father.

But Quinn Kelly was already pushing back his chair and sneaking outside. Dylan nodded to his parents' butler, James, to make sure the old man wasn't sneaking outside for a cigar.

Dylan sat forward and ran a hand over his mouth. He'd always thought them a tight-knit family. Until a few months back, on the night of his father's seventieth birthday, when they'd discovered a secret that threatened to knock their foundations out from under them.

His father, the true king behind the Kelly Investment Group, the powerhouse who had made their family the most influential in Brisbane, a man they had all thought might defy the odds and live forever, had serious heart problems that had led to him being brought back to life twice.

That night they had closed ranks, and told no one—for the sake of the financial stability of the business, and for the sake of their father's health.

Dylan's position as guardian of the parts of his family's lives deemed not fit for public consumption had only become all the more critical overnight.

It was a job he was more than happy to do. A job he'd needed to do since that long-ago day when the whole city had woken up to find their newspapers filled with pages dedicated to the gory specifics of the horrifically messy breakdown of his engagement.

If he'd been any other jilted man, with any other surname, nobody would have given a hoot. He'd realised that day the precarious position his whole family was in, and he'd taken it upon himself to be all of their safeguards against menace, exposure and innuendo.

Once James came back and intimated that Quinn was not disobeying doctor's orders, Dylan was able to relax. He shook off the dark memories of that long-ago, cloistered version of himself and glanced down the table to find his youngest brother, Cameron, and his new bride, Rosie, finishing off a bottle of wine, not even realising everyone else had gone.

A couple of minutes went by before Dylan realised he was still watching them.

His back teeth clenched and he downed the last swig of

Scotch in the glass held tight in his fist. Of all of his family he got on best with Cam—he was a sharp guy, and he wished him all the luck in the world. But in the back of his mind he worried for him. Odds were Rosie would turn out *not* to be the woman Cam thought she was.

'Aren't they just the sweetest things you've ever seen?'

Dylan blinked, and turned to find his mother standing behind him, a beatific smile on her face.

He stood and turned his back on the couple, hoping not having them in his sights might make the discomfort behind his ribs go away.

'So sweet my teeth hurt. Now when are you going to realise having us over is not akin to a state dinner? You can keep the Wedgwood in the cupboard. Bring out the Ikea flatware for us next time.' He kissed his mum on the cheek, and walked away, hoping to make a stealthy exit.

He headed through the drawing room only to find Brendan sitting at a table with a desk lamp, reading over some contract or other. He'd always been a workaholic, but even more so now that he was secretly running KInG while Quinn was forcibly sitting in his office playing solitaire all day instead of running the multibillion-dollar company that had likely taken ten years off his life in the first place.

Dylan stuck his hands in his trouser pockets and watched his brother a moment longer.

Brendan had been in a long-term relationship himself once, and had been left deeply hurt and alone. True, Chrissy had died unexpectedly, leaving him with two gorgeous young daughters to help fill the gap, both of whom were upstairs now, sleeping like angels, but Dylan still felt an empathy with the guy. If Brendan took a moment to bend, or appear even slightly less than indestructible, maybe they could be stalwarts together, resiliently emancipated from the burden of needing love.

'So that disturbance today,' Brendan said, causing Dylan to leap out of his skin. 'I assume you cleaned it up.'

'Assume away.'

Brendan managed to hold his breath for about three and a half seconds before closing the contract and looking up. 'I saw the news. Handcuffs? Seriously?'

Dylan grinned. He couldn't help himself. Hearing the word *'handcuffs'* come out of his stiff older brother's mouth was almost worth the afternoon chasing the owner of the handcuffs around the deep dark recesses of his mind.

He leant against a twelve-foot bookcase and crossed one ankle across the other. 'Her name's Wynnie. She wants us to help her save the world. I offered to take her to the moon and back instead.'

Brendan frowned even more than usual. 'You didn't—'

'Hey, a good time with me and she'll have trouble remembering her own name.'

Brendan rubbed his fingers over his eyes. 'Why, oh, why did she have to be a woman?'

Dylan grinned. 'It was a fifty-fifty chance and the gods love me.'

When Brendan looked as if he was about to burst a blood vessel Dylan sat in a chair across from him and filled him in on the specifics—Wynnie's new position, the details of her pitch, and the fact that she would not be getting back into the building any time soon.

'The deal wasn't worth considering?' Brendan asked.

'The deal was probably fine. But I have no intention of dealing with someone who all but blackmailed me into giving her the meeting in the first place. It's not a precedent I believe we want to set.'

Brendan's hard face softened into what looked to be the beginnings of a smile. 'You want her to know you're the biggest baddest image manipulator in town, not her.'

Dylan just stared back.

And Brendan shook his head as he opened the contract up again and began to read as he spoke. 'A Trojan horse, that's what she was. Letting her in the building was as good as admitting defeat. But if you think it's best to keep her at bay, then fine. That's the end of that.'

Dylan stared at the ends of his fingernails so long he lost focus. That was the end of that. No more Wynnie Devereaux. No more meetings, no more sightings, no more thinking about her.

Or her tousled hair. Or sweet-smelling skin. Or the blaze of attraction that had grabbed him and not let him go. Or the fact that while she claimed her name wasn't French her accent did have the sexiest tinge of European schooling about it. Or that he'd never met anyone, not even within his own boisterous gutsy family, who had the gumption to put their own pride, their own self-interest, a mile down the line behind standing up for what they believed in.

And she had promised she wasn't yet done with him. He wondered what other surprises she might have in store for him beneath her tough outer layer. Beneath that so-close-to-see-through-it-hurt top, beneath those tight white pants that left little to the imagination, beneath that delicate G-string—

'Another drink, sirs?' James asked from the doorway.

Brendan shook his head without looking up.

While Dylan dragged himself from the chair with a loud oomph. 'Not for this little duck. I'm home to bed.'

He slapped James on the shoulder as he passed. 'You'll keep an eye on them for me, won't you, James? Make sure they don't burn the manor down, or get caught in public naked, or do anything else I would have to clean up in the press the next day?'

'Always, Master Dylan.'

'Good man.'

CHAPTER FOUR

WYNNIE'S knee jiggled and her eyes hurt from staring agitatedly at the sun-drenched glass front of the Morningside café.

Her wrist ached from whipping her chai latte for the past ten minutes. To be more specific, the *muscles* ached. Her handcuff injuries were still swathed in bandages and magic cream; hence the need for a long-sleeved leather jacket over her black and white striped T-shirt.

Her eyes swept past warm orange walls, mismatched wooden chairs and deep purple couches as she glanced at the flat-screen TV on the wall behind the counter. A frothy current-affairs morning show was on, and in the bottom right-hand corner of the screen it told her she'd spent twelve minutes staring. Waiting. Knee-jiggling.

That was twelve extra minutes she could have slept. Twelve extra minutes in which she might have found time to cover the panda patches under her eyes and done something with her hair rather than just run hopeful fingers through it in the cab.

Brisbane's balmy weather, that was what had kept her awake the past few nights. Years spent in more reasonable, temperate climes meant her system was reeling from a little heat shock. Watching the fan spin above her bed, casting long shadows across the moonlit ceiling, while her hot, spreadeagled body took every whisper of shifting air it could, she had finally fallen asleep some time just before sunrise.

Her night sweats had had nothing to do with the fact that she knew that at seven-thirty this morning she'd be sitting in this very café awaiting the arrival of Dylan Kelly.

She looked to the TV again, and suddenly there she was in all her handcuffed glory. A static image over the newsreader's left shoulder spun to fill the screen showing her strapped to the inane sculpture while Dylan Kelly paced about her like a lion baiting his prey.

It was said that a camera added ten pounds. On Dylan Kelly wherever the camera had added bulk, it had worked. She shuffled on her seat, heat rising up her back, slithering behind her knees, pooling between her breasts.

She, on the other hand, with the wind flapping at her hair, and in her fanciful floral top, her knees knocking, her eyes locked in on Dylan's every move, did appear the 'eco-warrior' each outlet had labelled her. She wondered which one had written the wire and which others had barely bothered changing a word.

Either way, the term didn't sit well with her at all. It conjured up images of red paint-bombs, and angry protestors and tear gas.

And Felix. The last time she'd seen him at seventeen years old, he'd had the gleam of battle in his eye as he'd excitedly told her he was in Brisbane to protest with a group of mates. She'd been so proud of his passion. Little had she imagined the extent of the collateral damage involved in the war he had been about to wage, all in the name of the environment.

Her hand went straight for her mum's butterfly clip, today attached to the band of her watch.

Her family hadn't been brought up that way. Their focus had been living off the land, and leaving as small a mark upon it behind them as possible. It helped forge a more intimate community better connected to the world around them.

Finding a way to give the rest of the world just a taste of that idyllic existence was what she was working so hard to achieve now.

The café door swung inwards, a blinding flash of sunlight reflected off the angled glass and into her eyes.

A male form burst into the space, but she knew in an instant it wasn't the male form she sought. It was a more slightly built, younger man in a suit, talking non-stop into a mobile phone.

Her spine relaxed and she reached for her glass— Her fingers curled into her palm before she reached it.

The young man wasn't alone. He held open the door deferentially, and in his wake came another. Pale grey suit, white and grey striped shirt, no tie, platinum-framed sunglasses, broad shoulders, short dark blond hair, a chiselled jaw and lips built for sin. Head down, reading a newspaper held in one hand, this male seemed to suck every ounce of sunshine from the bright room.

As he moved away from the door the light redispersed itself into a more normal pattern and Dylan Kelly came into focus.

No more trying to tell herself that heatstroke had caused the sexual overdrive that had overcome her the last time they'd met. It was all him. She picked up her drink, downing the cooled muck in one hit.

All that was just too damned bad. This meeting was all about the work. It was her second take at chip, chip, chipping away at his rock-hard veneer.

He lifted his head as though he'd only just realised where he was. The man at his side, whom she now recognised as his assistant Eric, mimed that he would get the coffees. Dylan nodded once, then his eyes swept the room.

An equal mix of anticipation and trepidation slid through her body as she waited for him to catch her eye. Dylan wasn't exactly expecting her. She'd started off with the heroine-on-the-train-tracks approach, this time she was going with the sudden-leap-from-behind-a-tree attack.

Then suddenly she wondered if he'd even recognise *her* if he did spot her. What if she'd built up their first meeting into some kind of rare, mythical, sexual awakening when for him she'd been one of a dozen crazies he'd dealt with that day?

The urge to dive beneath the low coffee table nudging at her calves was a strong one…until his head stopped its slow perusal of the room so quickly his cheek clenched, and the newspaper in his hand crumpled beneath a tensed fist.

She took a deep breath and said, 'Here we go again,' beneath her breath, before giving him a jaunty wave.

Eric appeared at his side, noticed Dylan had turned to stone, then followed the direction of his gaze. When Eric saw her with her hand raised, the colour drained from the poor guy's face.

It wasn't as though she'd expected a big hello and a kiss on the cheek from Dylan, but brutal exasperation radiated from his entire body. Pesky as her job meant she could be, she'd never brought about that kind of intense reaction in another person before.

He reached up and slid off his sunglasses. The hit of those glinting blue eyes felt like a sucker punch to the stomach, even this time, when she ought to have been expecting it. Or perhaps that was her very problem. The expectation of seeing him again, of wondering if her reaction to him would be as outrageously vivid as the last time, had grown exponentially with every passing hour since she'd last walked away.

She stood, and waved an arm towards the matching couches surrounding the low-slung coffee table she'd secured for their 'meeting'. This time she'd had two days in which to get completely ready. She had all the information she needed right in front of her—statistics, research, cost-projections. And since the emails she'd sent had bounced, she had pamphlets, proposals and contracts at her fingertips.

Dylan's cheek twitched.

Wynnie's stomach rolled over on itself. Time slowed to a

most painful rate. Her jacket began to feel like a hotbox.
Come on, she begged inside her head.

And then he smiled. Wide lips. Straight white teeth. His
cheeks lifting to create half a dozen deep creases around
each blue eye.

When his smile turned to laughter, she called out across the
cafe, 'What?'

He began snaking around the haphazard tables in between
them until they were separated by the coffee table alone.

'What?' she said again.

'You.'

'Me what?'

'You are one tenacious woman, Miss Devereaux.' His smile
eased until it was all in his eyes.

As she drowned in a sea of sky blue, her neck relaxed and
her muscles grew loose. Loose enough she smiled right on
back. 'The sooner you realise I'm not going away, the sooner
you'll stop ignoring me.'

He tossed his sunglasses onto the couch and shucked off
his jacket, his shoulder muscles bunching and shifting beneath
his light cotton shirt. 'I'm afraid I couldn't ignore you even if
I wanted to. We'll be sitting here today, Eric,' he said, and
Wynnie glanced over his shoulder to see his assistant hovering.

'Sure thing, boss,' he said, then scurried off to grab their order.

Not quite believing her luck, Wynnie waited until Dylan
sat before sitting again herself. Her knees knocked as she
leant over to neaten up her presentation and the fabric of her
skinny jeans rubbing together sent hot sparks up her legs.

What with her leather jacket, her hot jeans, the chai latte
in her belly and Dylan Kelly smouldering at her three feet
away, she was very much in danger of heatstroke.

She ran a hand across her forehead to find it was moist.
Deciding it was better to appear foolish than to faint, she took
off her jacket and all but whimpered with pleasure when her
arms were bare to the blissful air-conditioning.

Unfortunately it took Dylan half a second to reach out and grab her hands. 'Now what the hell have you gone and done to yourself?'

Despite the lightning speed of his grab, he held her wrists gently, turning them over in his large hands, running his long fingers over the edge of the bandages. His face was so grave her heart skipped a beat.

When storm clouds began to gather in his eyes, she buckled. 'It was the handcuffs. They were cheap. They flared up a latent nickel allergy. I have to put on stupid cortisone cream three times a day. Happy now?'

So happy he burst into laughter. Peals of loud, free, pulsing laughter. Half the café stopped talking and stared. Everyone recognised him. If not as Dylan Kelly then likely as the guy who got coffee there every morning at seven-thirty. Those who did recognise him as Dylan Kelly quickly slid their eyes to her, the woman who had made him laugh.

She felt darts of envy impale her from about seven different points in the café. If they had any clue he had only laughed at her because she had made a fool of herself, rather than from any kind of friendliness, they might not feel so darkly towards her.

She sat on her hands. 'Are you done?' she asked between her teeth.

'For now,' he said, shifting on his seat and crossing his right foot atop his left knee. 'Now to what do I owe this unexpected pleasure? Or am I to suppose that it is pure coincidence that you are in this exact place at this precise time of day?'

'Mr Kelly—'

'Dylan. If this is to be our second shared coffee, I'd suggest the time has come for us to be more…familiar with one another.'

If she hadn't been on the receiving end of irritation in those daring blue eyes as many times as she already had, she might have thought he was suggesting something altogether more… familiar than he really was.

He was a man with a limited attention span.

She grabbed a hunk of papers from in front of her and said, 'I'm here to give you specifics on how our plan would work.'

'Well, isn't that a great pity?' he said.

And for a moment, taking in the rich timbre in his voice, and a flare of rare warmth in his eyes, she believed him. She blinked, yet felt it still. She breathed deep enough to catch his scent above the sugar and coffee flavours filling the air—

'Sorry it took so long,' a strange voice said instead, cutting so cruelly into her thoughts. 'They forgot your cinnamon again.'

The bustle at the edge of her vision pulled her gaze from Dylan's deep blue eyes to find Eric had joined them, was making a little table picnic for Dylan with coffee, sugar, napkin, spoons and a decadent-looking cream bun.

Once settled in the tub chair at the end of the coffee table, Eric pulled out a tiny laptop, sat it on his knees and looked to Wynnie in expectation.

When she looked back at Dylan, he had his newspaper in one hand, a coffee in the other, and to all intents and purposes he seemed to have forgotten she was even there.

She threw her papers onto the coffee table and thought about leaving. Giving up. Moving on to a new target, or maybe a new city. This was just too hard. Trying to work with this man was proving to be beyond her capabilities.

She closed her eyes tight.

And that was exactly why she had to see it through to the very end. Nothing was worth having if it wasn't a struggle to achieve. The reward at the end would only be greater for the blood, sweat and tears she gave to the endeavour. Maybe this was exactly what she needed to overcome to clear her conscience once and for all.

So she clasped her hands atop her knees and turned to Eric.

'Hi,' she said, offering him a friendly smile.

'Hello.'

Well, so far, in comparison with his astonishingly charismatic boss, he was…not exactly riveting. She managed to not look at Dylan, though she just knew he was smiling.

She had to get to the crunch, and forge a relationship with her new target, and fast.

'Eric, right? I'm Wynnie.'

'I know.'

Dylan's cheek twitched as he flapped the paper loudly and settled back into his seat to read the back sports page.

She leant towards Eric, but not close enough to scare the guy; he seemed a tad skittish. 'I love your suit. What's it made of?'

When he gawped at her, she slowly reached out and ran two fingers down the lapel. 'Worsted wool, right? Perfect choice for Brisbane weather.'

'Unlike leather,' Dylan murmured without looking up.

Wynnie nudged her jacket aside with her knee, and turned the full force of her charm back to Eric, who had at least managed to stop looking so bug-eyed.

'Do you live near here, too?' she asked.

He flicked a glance at his boss, who rolled his eyes in response before waving a defeated hand.

'Chapel Hill,' Eric said.

Having only lived in her uni town for a few months several years ago, her geography was a tad shaky, but Chapel Hill was on the bus route from the big draughty old house she'd shared with Hannah and a half-dozen others while at university.

'But that's a half-hour drive from here!' She poked a thumb in Dylan's direction. 'Does he make you drive all this way every morning to order his coffee?'

Eric's chest puffed out. 'I'm happy to do it.'

'By that he means no, I don't make him drive all this way,' Dylan drawled as he glanced her way. 'The kid's enthusiastic. Something you two have in common.'

Wynnie scowled. Eric blushed. And Dylan's long stare had her blood thrumming.

He wasn't generally nice. He didn't have any kind of natural inclination to do the right thing by the world at large. He was stubborn, antagonistic, cynical and infuriating. Yet she desperately, deplorably, immediately wanted to sleep with him. A futon, a king-sized water bed, the coffee table digging into her calves. She didn't care where. She didn't care when. All she cared was that it would happen. It had to happen. Or she might never be able to think straight again.

Maybe it was his very decadence that grabbed her so hard. His very wrongness and badness. Like her latent nickel allergy, his type was an itch she'd had her whole life that only now had been brought to the surface by circumstance.

Wynnie Gracious Devereaux Lambert, she yelled inside her head. *Present your pitch, get the hell out of here, then get thee to a yoga mat, or better yet an ice bath*!

'So, Eric,' she said, her voice sounding as unnaturally tight as her body felt, 'has Dylan filled you in on our plans?'

'My plan,' Dylan interjected, 'was to read the paper in peace. Your plans are yours alone.'

If only he knew exactly what she'd spent the past minute planning in precise detail!

She crossed her legs the other way so that her body faced Eric, then picked up a simple bulleted list typed on recycled paper. 'We can start out by focusing on simple insulation tricks, lessening plastic waste, paper waste, electrical waste and putting into place greener working methods for the future.'

Like a good little assistant Eric took the page and read it over. 'Seems easy enough,' he said with a nod.

She shot a testing look at Dylan. 'Doesn't it just?'

Dylan lifted his large *paper* cup to his lips and took a long swig. Wynnie found herself concentrating on his long fingers instead. Fingers that had stroked her breast, touched her lower back, caressed her sore wrists, and a hell of a lot more than that in her dreams.

She lifted her eyes to his to find his drinking had stilled and he was watching her. If her pupils weren't the size of dollar coins she had been let off lightly.

'Eric,' he barked and her list fluttered from the kid's hand to the table as though it had burnt his fingers.

'Yes, Mr Kelly.'

'I have the horrible feeling I left the iron on.' Dylan dangled his house keys at the young man.

Eric was on his feet in a second, and gone in another, leaving Wynnie and Dylan alone in the cosy corner of the café.

The clatter of laptop keys, the rich smell of really good coffee, the hiss of steaming milk all became heightened as Wynnie's senses went on full alert.

As did the realisation that below the table Dylan's foot was about an inch from her own, and that through the entire encounter with Eric and the keys Dylan's eyes had never once left hers.

She reached for her cup to find it had been taken by a waitress when she hadn't been paying attention. So she looked away instead, anywhere but at his deep, confusing, confronting, tempting blue eyes.

There were people everywhere—mums with prams, school kids with backpacks, other men and women in suits getting an early start to their days.

Nothing nefarious could happen here.

She relaxed enough to say, 'You think you left the *iron* on?'

Dylan's intimate, rumbling laughter filled the air and everyone else in the room faded away. 'He's dedicated, and consistent, and likeable, but so damn eager he never questions me. The day he does is the day he'll move up in the company.'

'So why did you send him away?'

Dylan folded over his broadsheet and placed it on the table. He leant forward and she breathed in a nose full of his clean, tangy scent. 'You're not going to get to me through Eric.'

She wrapped her hands about her knees, lest she give into temptation and reach out and stroke the hard edge where his cheek met his chin. But her voice was still giveaway husky as she asked, 'Then how *am* I going to get to you?'

His eyes darkened, his neck tensed and his nostrils flared as he took in a long slow breath. 'That's not your problem, Miss Devereaux. You get to me. Far more than I wish you did.'

She felt it then, as if she was being dipped slowly into a deep hot bath—the sling and slide of mutual sexual awareness.

When she'd thought it had just been her, that had been discomforting enough, but to know, without a doubt, that she brought out a rumble in his voice, a heaviness in his eyes, and who knew what other physical responses, made the ground beneath her feet no longer feel quite so stable.

She breathed in slowly so that he would not pick up on the trembles running through her, and she pretended to misunderstand.

'Then let me in,' she said. 'Let my people in. We can do it in secret. At night. With your people on top of us every step of the way. Let us see how you operate, allow us to come up with a plan to do it greener, and you will be shocked at how cost effective, and beneficial those changes will be in the short and long term. From the extra pride your staff will take in your workplace all the way to how your clients and your city perceive you. If you just opened yourself up to the possibility one tiny little bit, you'd see how perfect we are for one another.'

When his eyes turned dark as night she qualified, 'How perfect the CFC and KInG are for one another.'

His eyes remained locked on hers—hot, dark, as focused as she'd ever seen them. 'Wynnie, you are wasting your time tilting at the wrong windmill.'

She leant right forward, not caring how deeply into his personal space she'd gone. 'What can I say or do to make you change your mind?'

The words 'I'll do anything' seemed to cling to the air between them. Though she hadn't said them, hadn't really thought them, she wondered if the time might be nigh that it all mattered so much that she'd mean them.

His jaw clenched, and his eyes flickered at the ceiling. Then eventually he said, 'All the statistics in the world won't convince me. I'm no pen-pusher, or cheque-signer like those you've come up against before. Think of me as a pit-bull guarding the gates of my family lore. Push me too hard, take one step too close, and I will bite.'

'I'm pushing too hard,' she said, her voice catching on the final word as she found herself caught in the rare moment of candour in his unpredictable eyes.

He nodded, and seemed to lean nearer to her still. His shirt bunched into waves against his stomach muscles. The tendons in his hands stood out in tanned ridges as though he, too, was holding himself at bay.

'I'm getting too close?' She was asking herself as much as she was asking him.

One of his hands braced the coffee table, resting mere millimetres from hers on her knees. If she took too deep a breath their fingers would touch.

'Wynnie, you've been too close since the moment you set foot on my forecourt.'

Wynnie felt the air between them contract and pulse. She took a deep breath through her nose and it bled from her mouth in a most unsteady exhale.

Before she had the chance to come up with anything sophisticated or coherent in response, Dylan's hand slipped away, reached into his trouser pocket and pulled out his phone, which he pressed to his ear. She hadn't even heard it ring.

'Kelly,' he said, his eyes not leaving hers. But as the seconds passed the clarity therein slowly, eventually, completely dispersed. They lit with a glinting smile that, no matter how appealing, felt to her as though the shutters had come down with a clang.

'I can't remember,' he said into the phone, then flipped it

shut. 'That was Eric, wondering in which room I might have been using my iron.'

She slid her hands tight between her knees to stop them from tingling as though he were still close, still within reach. 'If you own an iron I'll walk out of here today and never bother you again.'

His eyes crinkled. 'To think, a hundred bucks' worth of electrical appliance is all it would have taken.'

He could have lied, and she could have gone through with her joke as though it had been a promise. But neither of them did either thing. They sat across from one another, turning a blind eye to their impasse.

She swept a glance to his phone, held between his hands so tight he could crush the poor thing. 'You should ring him back and tell him you were mistaken.'

Dylan slipped his phone back into his trouser pocket. 'Nah. He likes to feel useful.'

'I knew from the moment I met you that you were in league with the devil.'

His smile grew into a grin, but rather than making her head spin, it only made her feel oddly wistful. Now that she'd had a taste of the candour available to her behind the charming mask, the mask would never feel like enough.

Dylan stood and folded his paper beneath his arm. He glanced over her knocked knees, her messy hair and her bandaged wrists before he covered his eyes with his dark sunglasses.

She stood along with him. This was a business meeting after all. 'So I'm assuming today's not the day you're going to sign on with the CFC.'

'Afraid not.'

'Then let me give you one last thought to take away with you. When we run out of water, when your backyard backs onto landfill, when you have to wear a mask so as to breathe the air without choking, you'll be wishing you'd given the bothersome brunette her dues.'

He leant back on his heels, not flinching, not even moving. Until his mouth curved up into a smile. The kind of smile that made her breathe a little harder than normal. Made her heart feel a little more present in her chest.

And then he did the most unexpected thing. He picked up her proposal, and glanced at it for a moment. Just a moment, but it was the most amount of consideration he'd given her yet. Maybe she ought to have imperilled his backyard sooner.

She opened her mouth to tell him to take it with him, but with a shake of his head he let it flutter back to the table.

And this time she had to watch him walk away.

'Damn it,' she swore beneath her breath, kicking the edge of the heavy coffee table for good measure. It hurt her big toe, but it was worth it for the excess energy it sent somewhere other than her stormy stomach.

He claimed she'd pushed too hard, but the way she saw it if she wasn't getting through she wasn't pushing hard enough.

As to getting too close… The memory of the warmth in his eyes as he'd uttered those words washed over her in a flood of sexual awareness.

When he reached the café door he turned and looked her way one last time. At least her skin thrummed as though he had. With his eyes hidden behind those dark sunglasses she couldn't really be sure.

And her deepest instincts when it came to understanding the thoughts and hearts of men had been proven to be disastrously wrong before.

CHAPTER FIVE

THAT night, after everyone else in the office had gone home, Wynnie and Hannah sat on the edge of her glass desk at CFC headquarters.

Feeling like a wind-up toy that had never run out of puff, Wynnie clicked a fingernail manically against her top teeth, and Hannah swung her legs rhythmically beneath the desk as they both stared silently at Dylan's picture pinned to the back of her office door.

In the past few days, in moments when she had been particularly frustrated with him, or with herself, she'd drawn on a Groucho Marx moustache, a plethora of hooped earrings in one ear, a pirate's bandana, and a number of missing teeth.

But beneath the pen marks those blue eyes of his constantly shone through—gorgeous, audacious, mocking her, flirting with her, making her whole body feel as if it were wrapped in rubber bands.

'So he actually read the proposal?' Hannah asked.

'He glanced at it.'

'That's a good thing. A gal won't take a dress off the rack and check the price tag unless she likes the look of it in the first place.'

'Dylan Kelly's no gal.'

Hannah cocked her head as she looked back at the picture. 'No, he's not. And I'm not sure he'd buy off the rack, either.

But he looked. He touched. It's a sign you're getting through to him and that's a good thing.'

Wynnie sat on her hands. *The way he looked at her... The way he touched her.* That might have felt like a good thing, but it certainly was not.

She shook her head. 'More like a sign to say don't call me, I'll call you. Which translates even more specifically into leave me the hell alone before I get my big fancy lawyers to take out a restraining order.'

Hannah's legs stopped swinging beneath the desk, and she slowly turned to face her. 'So you think he's going to call you, huh?'

'I don't know why I bothered coming to you,' she said on a sigh as she slid off her desk, grabbed her purse and Hannah's arm and dragged her from the office and into the long, carpeted hallway lit only by the fluorescent green emergency signs.

Hannah linked her hand through Wynnie's elbow. 'Because I'm such a fun source of moral corruption. Now tell Auntie Hannah what's really bothering you.'

'Okay. I can't believe I'm about to say this. He acts like, well, not as though he likes me, but as though he's finding it really hard not to ravage me on the spot.' She held on to Hannah's arm and squeezed her eyes shut tight, feeling ridiculous now she'd said the words out loud. 'And I know that he's well-practised at the art, and he's likely had every other woman in town and that's the only reason I'm still on his radar, but, still, I can't help but feel it.'

'And this is a bad thing?'

'It makes it extremely difficult to focus.'

Hannah's laughter bounced off the windows and walls until it echoed inside Wynnie's head. She opened one eye.

'That's why they call him the smiling assassin,' Hannah said. 'He blinds with that beautiful face and body and voice and... Well, that's enough really. Then while you're drowning in his eyes he kills your proposal before you've even finished shaking his hand. It's kind of his MO.'

Wynnie let that sink in, all the way to her suddenly heavy toes. 'This is common knowledge? What the hell else are the CFC's researchers leaving out?'

Hannah smiled and nodded.

'And this is the man you all convinced me was the one *I* had to lobby? The same man you have continuously tried to convince me to ask out on a date?'

The nodding and smiling stopped as Hannah obviously saw her point. 'I'm a lawyer. It's my job to be able to argue both sides of the same point with equally compelling reason. Besides which, sweetie, you know better than most that a person's reputation is only a portion of their true self.'

Wynnie shook her head. This wasn't about her, it was about ruddy Dylan Kelly. 'You told me he was a rogue easily enough, why has it taken you until now to tell me *this* is his *business* reputation?'

Hannah sniffed. 'I'm no gossip.'

'Yes, you are!'

'You're right, I am. I truly thought we were mucking about. It never occurred to me that you might really be taken with him.'

'How can I not be? He's all I ever talk about at work, all I ever talk about with my media contacts. He and his business and his family are all I ever think about. I'm saturated by the guy.'

Hannah grinned. 'How much do I love that imagery? Now come on, my young friend, he is wealthy, influential, sexy, and available. If you cut out that entire group as possible dating material what are you leaving for yourself?'

'Helpful, thanks.'

'Hey, I'm a realist. Which is why I'm trying to save the planet, and also why I'm *not* going to rule out any cute guy just because I work with him, or just because he doesn't have the exact same beliefs as me, or just because he has eight toes on each foot.' Hannah jabbed a finger at the security doors. 'It happens.'

Just before the doors opened Wynnie caught her reflection in the glass—her eyes were wide and dark just from thinking about the guy. She was taken with him. But now she was coming to realise how much that sprang from his contradictions. He played the playboy with such panache, but it still couldn't hide the depth of his convictions, and his single-mindedness when it came to protecting his family.

The similarity to her own double life was stunning. How was a girl like her to resist?

They hit the Toowong street to find it bustling with late-night shoppers, locals strolling after eating out, and uni students herding towards the plethora of local pubs.

'So here's my two cents,' Hannah said, 'for which I'd actually charge four hundred dollars an hour if it was anyone else but you, so pay attention. You're a sweetheart and if you like him, then he has to be worth liking. If you're not yet sure if you can trust him, trust yourself.'

Trust. That was what this whole thing was about. Her rabid inability to trust anyone but herself. Hell, her trust in herself had been worn pretty thin, too. She didn't need a psychology degree to know it came from being let down in the worst possible way by the closest person to her in all the world.

The easy ability to love she'd had as a kid had been stripped away the second she'd opened the door of her Sociology 101 class to find herself face to face with the dean and a handful of policemen.

Too bad if she was coming to believe that deep down Dylan Kelly might actually be *decent*.

'What are you doing?' Hannah asked when she realised Wynnie had stopped walking.

'Waiting for the bus.'

'You do this every night?'

'Most.'

Hannah grabbed her by the sleeve and tugged her up the brightly lit street. 'You try too hard.'

'It has nothing to do with trying. I have no intention of hopping in a car every day if I don't even need to.'

Hannah shook her head. 'My car's gonna be guzzling gas anyway. I'll drive you home.'

'Fine. Just let's talk about something else for a while.'

Hannah linked her arm through Wynnie's once more. 'Ah, what fine weather we're having.'

Wynnie laughed. Brisbane almost always had fine weather. But playing along would serve her cause. 'We sure are.'

On Friday evening Dylan sauntered into his office, his eyes skimming over the below-the-fold article on the front page of *The Australian*, a paper cup of fresh coffee warming his other hand, when the hairs on the back of his neck told him he wasn't alone.

Jack Colby, an old school mate, and the best private investigator in the country, was sitting in his office chair, feet on his desk, ignoring the stunning, glittering night view of the Riverside Expressway and South Bank bordering the city straight of the Brisbane River.

'Evening, Jack,' he said.

Jack's silhouette nodded. 'Dylan. How's things?'

'The amount I pay you I'd hope you know the answer to that better than I.'

It took him a second to remember when and why he'd hired Jack this time around.

When? Days earlier. Why? Wynnie Devereaux.

From the moment he'd looked into those soft brown eyes down the lens of Eric's mate's camera he'd found himself in uncharted waters—torn between wanting to slap a restraining order against her stopping her from coming anywhere near his family, and wanting to immerse himself in the heat that flickered deep in her eyes every time they made contact with his, and wanting to do whatever he had to do to ease the aching vulnerability that engulfed her in moments when she let down her guard.

None of those courses of action was ideal so he'd needed to find another way to cut her off.

Since there was no way she was merely the frustratingly sexy tree-hugger she appeared to be, she had to have a hidden agenda, a self-serving reason why he was in her line of sight. They always did.

Indubitably once he knew exactly what her ulterior motives were, she would be rendered far less intriguing. Enter Jack.

Dylan closed his paper and threw it on the coffee table by the lounge suite in the corner. He undid the buttons at his wrists, rolled up his sleeves and dragged a tub chair over to the guest side of his desk.

'What've you got?'

Jack sat forward and opened up a slim, innocuous-looking Manila folder.

'Rightio. Wynnie Devereaux. Twenty-seven years old. Brunette. Brown eyes. Slim build. Average height. Single. Pretty girl.'

Jack didn't know the half of it. Her soft floral scent invaded Dylan's dreams. He could feel the warmth of her skin caressing his palms in the middle of business meetings. Every time he saw a woman with dark brown hair, anywhere, he found himself looking twice.

Dylan raised an eyebrow. 'I don't pay you to editorialise.'

Jack grinned. 'It's rare this job has such perks.' He slid a handful of photographs of her across the desk.

The first was Wynnie walking down a city street the day they'd first met. He'd recognise those thighs in those white pants anywhere. A curly-haired blonde was at her side, hands gesticulating.

As he moved through the photos Wynnie's face was serious, shocked, then laughing. Her wrists were bound in bandages. He ran a finger across his lips to stop from smiling.

In the final picture she seemed to be looking directly into the camera, her brow furrowed, her eyes determined, her dark hair whipping about her lovely face. Eyes like honey. Skin like cream. Her life force bursting from her every pore.

Dylan's whole hand rested across his mouth. If that was all Jack could get…

He threw the photos onto the desk. 'Nothing I didn't already know from just meeting her.'

'I was simply waiting until I had your attention.'

Dylan's eyes narrowed. 'You have it.'

'She studied a range of humanities on a scholarship at the University of Queensland when she was eighteen after being home-schooled her whole life, but didn't finish even a year. She moved to Paris before she turned twenty and once there talked her way into a job with a local parks beautification group.'

So that made sense of the faint accent at least.

'She's worked for numerous organisations since, raising funds, lobbying for government help, last of which was an Arena di Verona Restoration Committee. The money she raised and the profile she built for the Opera house would turn even you on a little bit.'

Dylan shifted in his chair. As if he needed another reason. 'That's it? She's a gifted twenty-seven-year-old lobbyist. You're slipping, my friend.'

Jack just leant back in his chair and grinned.

The hairs on the back of Dylan's neck stood to attention. There was more. And not just more. There was dirt. A valid reason for him to be on his guard and exceedingly wary of the vigorous way he reacted to her.

'One salient thing I might point out before you file that folder away,' Jack drawled.

'Spit it out.'

'Though Wynnie Devereaux is the name on her driver's licence, her passport, her Medicare card, her employment contracts, it's not her real name.'

Dylan placed a finger on the top photo, the one where he could look into her eyes. 'Then who the hell is she?'

Jack stood and cocked his hand into the shape of a pistol. 'I don't want to spoil all the surprises. The rest I'll let you read for yourself.'

He swept from his office, leaving Dylan with a bill, and the thin Manila folder that suddenly seemed a mile deep.

Dylan stared at it, unusually unwilling to dive right in. Because the truth of it was, even though he'd been the one to have her background plundered for dirt, for some ridiculous reason he'd half believed that maybe, just maybe, he'd met the last honest woman on the planet.

It seemed he'd been right all along. There was no such creature to be found.

He opened the folder, flicked through until he found the photocopy of an old news report, and began to read.

CHAPTER SIX

ON SATURDAY night Wynnie and Hannah's cab, a hybrid to keep them both happy, pulled up in front of the Queensland Museum at South Bank. The great hulking concrete and glass building was floodlit by blocks of pink and orange light, the pathway ahead swathed in pink and orange chiffon.

Through the car windows Wynnie watched women in glamorous, barely there, summertime evening dress and men in exquisite tuxedos slip from shiny black town cars that lined the street in front and behind them.

'Charity balls sure ain't what they used to be,' she said under her breath. 'It looks like an orgy waiting to happen.'

Hannah appeared at the window and Wynnie jumped. Then realised she was still inside the cab, whose driver was waiting for her to vamoose. She shot him a quick smile and hopped out, taking care to keep her knees locked as flash bulbs of paparazzi cameras did their all to catch her in a compromising position in case she was a somebody.

She held her sparkly silver purse in front of her face, ostensibly to shield her eyes from the lights, but more truthfully it was a move born of instinct.

Putting herself in the public eye she could handle. But the thousand flashes of a flock of rabid photographers crowding towards her, screaming her name, always took her right back to the time when she had been a 'person of interest' in the bombing of a uni science lab, walking from the police station a free woman but with the life she'd known in tatters at her feet.

Hannah grabbed her hand away from her face. 'I know I look super-hot tonight, but they don't know me from a bar of soap. You, Wynnie my sweet, they lurve. So for the sake of my standing with the bosses, for the sake of the money I spent on this dress, and by George, for the sake of the planet, smile for the cameras.'

Wynnie mentally slapped herself across the back of the head. She was no longer an ice-blonde with pixie-short hair. She no longer wore enough eyeliner to sink a ship. Ponchos and multi-coloured hemp flares were no longer her uniform of choice. And she'd lost the classic freshman fifteen pounds a long time ago.

So she smiled, she twirled, she tossed her hair. She waved to photographers and cameramen she'd met during her interviews so far. She gave pithy sound bites about the Clean Footprint Coalition to anyone with a recording device. And she thanked her lucky stars for cortisone now that her wrists were clear bar a slight pink ring that nobody would see unless they got really really close.

And she acted for all the world as though beneath her short, slinky tomato-red silk dress she had nothing to hide. Her arms were covered to her wrists, but her legs were bare to mid-thigh, and the thing slithered so close against every inch of her skin the world now knew she had an 'innie' for a belly button.

When they walked through the front doors her eyes almost popped out of her head. The long, thin, three-storey foyer was usually empty, bar stunning, life-sized models of a family of humpback whales suspended in the open space above. This night, bringing the same warm, decadent feeling from the outside inside, backlit swathes of pink and orange crêpe draped from the ceiling creating intimate, warm, rosy, golden light over the ornate, candlelit tables scattered throughout.

'Is there going to be any money left over to give to the charity?' Wynnie said out of the corner of her mouth.

'Not our charity tonight,' Hannah said, 'so not *our* concern. Just be grateful the head honchos love you so much they gave us these tickets, and remember we're here to get you some much-needed fun. To get some booze into you. Then a bit of dance-floor action when the party gets going. Maybe you'll even meet yourself a nice, cute, harmless yet wild-in-the-sack philanthropist. Because you can't stay wound up this tight or you're gonna pop. And there's nowhere in that dress for you to go.'

Hannah grinned, picked up the heavy tribal beat of the music booming through the lofty space and boogied away into the pulsating crowd.

But Wynnie's feet had stuck to the floor of the wickedly decorated foyer. She wished then that she'd worn a sack, or a large shawl or at the very least an entirely different dress.

For not ten feet in front of her, looking resplendent in an exquisite tuxedo, stood Dylan Kelly.

Not now, she thought, *not tonight*. Not when she still hadn't come to any logical, sensible, rational conclusions about what she could do with the feelings she had for the guy.

Still she couldn't take her eyes off him. Standing in a group of men about his age, all dressed much the same, all exuding that suave, easy, master-of-the-universe air that came of growing up blanketed by privilege, Dylan Kelly stood out as though he walked through life with a spotlight shining down upon him.

His dark blond hair looked darker, slicked back off his face. He had one hand in the pocket of his black trousers, pulling the seat firmly across a pinchable derrière. He pointed at something in the distance, stretching his snowy white shirt tight across his torso that made the very most of the kind of build that spoke of sit-ups and a lot of them.

Her mouth literally began to water.

As though someone had tapped him on the shoulder and

said 'she's here' Dylan glanced away from the group and his
eyes found hers. Hot, dark, stunning blue.

In a nervous gesture she couldn't control, her hand fluttered
to her hair, brushing against her butterfly clip tucked within
the waves. But rather than feeling grounded, she felt fragile,
breakable, small.

Without saying a word, Dylan left the group and made a
beeline towards her. The crowd parted. His gaze slunk down
one side of her underdressed body then up the other, leaving
a trail of enfeebling goose bumps in its wake.

As he came close enough she could pick out the scent of
his now all too familiar aftershave his eyes found hers. He
conjured the most charming half-smile as he drawled, 'Of all
the museums in all the world…'

Wynnie gripped her purse so tight sequins left tattoos on
her hot palms. 'Why, Dylan Kelly, what on earth is a man like
you doing in a place like this?'

He moved to stand beside her, clasping his hands behind
his back as he looked out over the crowd. 'Perhaps I knew
you'd be here tonight. Perhaps I've come to see the creature
in her own environment, mingling with her own species. Such
a scoop would certainly help me to learn a thing or two about
how to defend myself against you.'

Wynnie smiled and waved to a woman involved with solar
energy research whom she'd met through the CFC when she'd
first come to town. The woman waved back, though only after
fixing her hair in case Dylan's eyes turned her way, as well.

'You think you need help?' she muttered. 'Between you
and me you're doing a bang-up job so far.'

'One must always do what one can to do better.'

She glanced sideways to find he was no longer interested
in the crowd. His attention was one hundred per cent on her.

She said, 'It's fifteen hundred dollars per plate. That's an
expensive experiment.'

He leant in so close his breath tickled her hair against her ear. 'Somehow I get the feeling uncovering your layers will be worth every cent I've paid.'

Her knees buckled, and her airway all but closed up. Only years of lobbying men as intimidating and less likely to soften any disapproval with a gorgeous smile helped her get by without her voice giving her away. 'I'm sure you're quite aware that you could make an appointment to see me, in more layers than I am wearing tonight, at my office any time. Here, I would have thought the weight of do-gooderness in the air might cramp your style.'

'Nah,' he said, his voice dropping a note, maybe even two, 'my style will be just fine.'

He took a step closer as he looked back out into the seething, sparkling crowd. 'So, which of these poor schmucks do you plan on getting your claws into tonight?'

'It's my night off,' she shot back. 'I'm here to relax and have a nice time. You and your sort are safe from my sticky clutches.'

She felt his eyes on her again, but she knew better than to lock gazes at this proximity. She turned and backed away. 'Do me a favour?'

'Name it.' Dylan slid a hand back into the pocket of his trousers. Wynnie did her best to keep her gaze on his receding face.

'These good people are here tonight because they care about clean energy and that's why *they've* paid good money to be here. Try not to rub off on them.'

And then he laughed. Head back, rumbling laughter that from deep within his belly. Heads turned, all female.

But Dylan's eyes remained fixed entirely on her. 'Wynnie,' he called out, not caring a lick who heard, 'I could ask the same of you. But then we'd both be disappointed.'

The further she backed away, the more the burgeoning crowd surged between them. His laughter, and his smile and the intense electricity that surged through her with simply being near the guy, gradually dimmed to a sweet buzz.

'You'll get a neck crick,' Hannah said.

Wynnie came back to the present to find the Minister for the Environment, Heritage and the Arts had finished his speech and a jazz band had struck up a soft shuffle on stage. She was sucking air through a straw as her mocktail was empty bar crushed ice and lime pulp, and she was staring at the back of Dylan's head as three tables over he had a dozen people in stitches.

Placing the offending glass on the pink tablecloth, Wynnie spun on her seat and glanced at Hannah who was grinning at her over a mouthful of caramel tart.

Wynnie said, 'I know I am officially off the clock, but this is my first opportunity to watch the guy interact with his peers. If I'm going to win him over, I need all the help I can get.'

Hannah laid a hand on Wynnie's wrist. 'If that's the line you're sticking with, then more power to you.'

Wynnie shook out her shoulders and spooned a mouthful of mocktail-flavoured crushed ice from the bottom of her glass before a liveried waiter swept it away.

'Wynnie,' a deep familiar voice said from behind her, 'may I have a word?'

And she almost choked on the ice.

Hannah's chair squeaked loudly against the stone floor. Wynnie, coughing, glanced across to find Hannah had leapt to her feet with her hand outstretched while somehow, simultaneously, leaving barely any daylight between her body and Dylan's.

'Hannah Laskowski,' she breathed huskily. 'It's a pleasure to make your acquaintance.'

Dylan, ever the coolest man on the planet, managed to smile as if he meant it. He took Hannah's hand. 'Dylan Kelly, the pleasure is mine.'

'I'm Wynnie's boss. Sort of. So anything you have to say to her, you can say to me. Here, or elsewhere.'

Wynnie suddenly felt her chair sliding backwards and she had to stand or fall flat on her butt. She spun, and released a loud 'oomph' as she smacked into Dylan who, it turned out, had been the one pulling her chair out from under her.

She grabbed tight to his velvet soft lapels to stop from falling in a heap. He slid an arm around her waist for the same reason. *Funny*, she thought, blinking into his blue eyes, *it doesn't feel like he's trying to keep me from falling at all*.

He said, 'Thanks for the offer, Hannah, but I prefer to keep my business contacts close. The wider the spread, the more chance things can get lost in translation.'

'Fine with me!' Hannah said. Wynnie shot a look over her shoulder to find her friend grinning like a proud fairy godmother.

Wynnie was frowning by the time she glanced back at Dylan. 'Hannah knows the word *"no"* in as many languages as I do. What on earth could get lost in translation?'

His arm slid tighter still, pressing her hips against his with such force her head rocked back. 'Come with me and you'll find out.'

His spare hand found one of hers and soon she was being pulled in his wake. She turned back to Hannah for help, but her friend was sitting at the table, resting her cheek on her palm and licking the last drop of liquid off the end of a flamingo-shaped swizzle stick.

'Mr Kelly,' she said, smiling at those she wriggled to avoid as they surged through the crowd. 'Dylan!'

He stopped so suddenly she slammed into him again. This time she reached out and pushed against his chest before she ended up in his arms.

'Yes, Wynnie.'

'You said you had something you wanted to talk about.'

'I did, didn't I?'

'So talk.' She crossed her arms, and stuck a high-heel-clad

foot out in front of her, pointy toe up, keeping a healthy gap between them.

Still he managed to grab her hand, spin her out and draw her back in close, right as the band started playing 'The Way You Look Tonight'.

'What are you—?'

'Shut up and dance or everyone will stare.'

'Considering we are the only ones on the dance floor,' she hissed, 'everyone is already staring.'

'Then we may as well make the most of it.'

Dylan tucked her close, moving her around the dance floor as though he were on wheels. She gave in and followed as best she could, and soon the crowd faded away as his clean scent, his hard body, his gentle embrace served to fill up every ounce of room her mind had on offer.

She was adrift on a cloud of pure pleasure when the fingers of his left hand wound around her wrist before sliding back up to wrap about her right hand.

'All better?' he asked.

'So long as I keep away from cheap handcuffs I should be fine.'

'I can give you the line on where to find a more respectable brand. If the need ever arises.'

She shot him a sarcastic smile. 'I have no doubt.'

He ducked her under his arm, slid her around his back, and she was in his arms again before she even knew what was happening.

'Smooth,' she said, a tad breathless and not from the exercise. The guy could really dance. And he was smooth. Of course he was, he was perfect—perfectly bred, perfectly arrogant, perfectly oblivious to what someone with his infamy could do to look out for not only those closest to him, but his whole community.

He even smelled perfect.

'Did you say something?' he asked.

She tensed, slowing him down to a soft shuffle so she

could extricate herself before she did something really stupid like leaning her head on his shoulder and sighing.

'Won't your date wonder why you're not out here with her?' she asked.

'No date tonight.'

Her flicker of a glance took in at least half a dozen women watching him from the sidelines looking ready to pounce. 'I imagined you the type to have a little black book the thickness of *War and Peace*.'

His smile was breathtaking. 'I gave the inhabitants a night off.'

'How magnanimous.'

He offered a shallow bow, and the look in his eyes when they found hers again was anything but magnanimous.

The exact reflection of her own absorbing attraction in his eyes might have been real or imagined. It didn't matter. What mattered was how much she needed fresh air and for that she needed to be anywhere but in Dylan Kelly's addictive arms.

'Mr Kelly—'

'It was Dylan a moment ago.'

'Fine. Dylan, if your conscience has finally come to the party and you are ready to sit down with me, properly, and make a deal about how I can change the way you do business for the better—'

'That's a lot of weight for you to carry on such small shoulders,' he said, his hands running over them, his eyes following.

'That's why I need you to share it with me.'

His eyes shot to hers. Deep, reclusive, unreachable.

'One person can make a difference,' she said. 'A hundred people can change the world.'

'Mmm,' he rumbled in her ear as he pulled her close. 'So you keep telling me.'

Her rebellious body melted against him, softening to fit as closely as it possibly could without needing an X-rating.

He said, 'You know what?'

'What?'

'I'm not sure if it was the candlelight or the pink napkins that did it, but the minute I sat down to dinner my heart gave a little twinge I'd never felt before. An inner desire to legalise marijuana, and talk to dolphins, and throw cans of red paint at women in fur coats.'

Wynnie's melting body snapped upright. 'You're an ass.'

She pushed away. She tried to anyway. Dylan's will to hold her seemed to be stronger than hers to be free.

'Stay,' he said, his laughing voice low enough only she could hear. She imagined a lick of rawness. Of the sincerity she had only glimpsed on rare moments few and far between.

She glared at him, but her pushing didn't get any stronger. 'Give me one good reason why I shouldn't kick you in the shin and get back to my caramel tart.'

He took her back into a dance hold and began to sway, his hips sliding against hers, nothing between them but some ridiculously thin silk and tuxedo trousers. It took all of her energy to keep from whimpering.

'You think people are staring now?' he said. 'Walk off this floor before the song ends and our lovers' tiff'll be page three while the coverage of this here party, and any good will towards the charity, will be shunted twenty pages back. You don't want to be blamed for that, do you?'

'You *are* the devil,' she said. 'You know that, don't you?'

His smile was pure sin. 'I admit to nothing. Now stop fighting me. Dance.'

Wynnie took a deep fortifying breath which only pressed her chest flush against his. Not a good idea. Her breasts let her down; swelling, hardening, begging her to stay close to the wall of masculine heat.

She let her breath slowly go, and did her best to relax. There could only be seconds remaining of the song. Seconds for her to wonder what he was playing at. Because she knew as well as she knew her own name, well, both of them, that he wasn't dancing with her because he had finally realised he couldn't keep his hands off her. He had some new angle she couldn't hope to fathom.

The only angle she had the chance to discover was the new angle of his hips as he slid his knee gently between hers. And finally she was undone. Fighting him was all too hard when compared with just giving in.

Her eyes fluttered shut and her breath expelled from her lungs in a soft sigh.

His hand slid lower down her back, the silk of her dress slithering across her skin, and tiny prickles of sweat sprang up in its wake. She didn't have time to worry, for that was when he somehow tipped her off balance. Her left leg gripped his and suddenly she was arched back into a low dip.

There they stayed. One bar. Two.

Her breaths came heavily. The faint edge of a not so recent shave leant shadows to his carved cheeks. A muscle twitched therein. His eyes narrowed. Darkened. His grip on her hand tightened.

Trust. Bad judgment. Decency. Decadence. The survival of the planet. None of it mattered in that moment as much as the fire in his eyes.

The song came to an end. Then she was upright again. Their heavy breaths intermingled as their chests heaved against one another. Every place their bodies had touched felt aflame. Every place they hadn't longed to do so. Suddenly the idea of being on page three of the paper didn't matter a lick. If he leant in, if he closed the gap, if he pressed his lips to hers—

'Kelly,' a loud unfamiliar voice said. 'Thought that was you.'

Wynnie blinked and realised they were no longer alone. In fact, the dance floor was full of couples clapping the band. A gentleman reached past her to shake Dylan's hand, slap him on the back, sequester his attention.

She slipped out of his embrace, ran shaking hands down her dress and put enough space between them that she could breathe.

His eyes were still dark, and still fully trained on her as the gent shouted about market forces and the Dow Jones and some celebrity golf tournament he'd paid a fortune for at some auction.

A Violent Femmes classic started up and the crowd went wild, jumping up and down, rocking the room. Wynnie offered Dylan a slight shrug, then, taking her chance, she slipped away, trying to concentrate on protecting her peep toes from bouncing stiletto heels, when she could still feel Dylan's eyes on her back as she pressed through the boisterous crowd.

With each step away she tried to shake off the feeling that rather than dancing just now she'd actually been tiptoeing around the edge of a volcano.

Only once she was free of the crowd and was heading through the now mostly empty tables back towards her seat did she realise whatever it was Dylan had intended to say to her had never been said.

Then again, maybe the dance had said it all.

Wynnie stood in the corner of the museum foyer, on her tippy toes, trying to spy Hannah's blonde curls from amidst the slick-dos, wishing the girl hadn't had one too many cocktails or her goodbyes would take forever.

'Well, if it isn't Guinevere Lambert.'

She landed back on her heels with a thud, kept her eyes dead ahead and swallowed as discreetly as she could while she pretended that she hadn't just heard someone use her real name.

A body slid in beside her. It felt big and tall and male. It smelt like cigarette smoke and too many hours spent wearing the same clothes.

'It is Guinevere, isn't it? I saw you earlier with Kelly on the dance floor and something pinged in the back of my head. I couldn't place you and then suddenly…there it was. Ten odd years ago. Sweet, little, hippy waif Guinevere Lambert, chin up, lips sealed, surrounded by the boys in blue as they led you from your uni class and all the way to police central.' He held out a hand smack bang in the middle of her personal space. 'Garry Sloane. Allied Press Corps.'

She glanced down at the hand to find it held a digital voice recorder the size of a tube of lipstick. She bit her lip, and pressed her feet hard into the harder floor to stop herself from trembling. She wouldn't lie to the guy, in the end that would serve no purpose but to make sure she never worked in public relations ever again. But neither did she have a clue what to say.

Where the hell was Hannah? She'd said she'd be two minutes!

'Sloane, leave the lady alone.'

Wynnie looked up to find the big man at her side was being overshadowed by an even bigger man. One with pure venom lighting the depths of his dark blue eyes.

'Kelly,' Sloane said. 'This has nothing to do with you or your darling family. So why don't you sashay on away and leave me and this nice lady to our conversation?'

When the reporter turned to face Wynnie she was caught looking him in the eye. His weathered face broke into the kind of expression that ought never to be allowed to be called a smile. 'Am I right?' he asked.

She stared at him, and narrowed her eyes. He was right about one thing—what he wanted to talk to her about had nothing to do with Dylan and neither did she want it to.

She turned to Dylan, and had to swallow before she could manage a word. 'I'm fine.'

He glanced at her throat, which was still working hard to get any kind of moisture to her poor mouth, then back into her eyes. Whatever he saw there had him ignoring every word she said.

'Nevertheless,' Dylan growled, 'I think you wouldn't find it hard to track down cockroaches more worthy of talking to.'

Sloane puffed out his chest and Wynnie had the distinct feeling that this no longer had anything to do with her.

'Surely,' Sloane hissed, 'you of all people know better than to rub me the wrong way.'

'Go,' Dylan said, his voice as cold as ice. 'Now. Out of my sight. Before I do something you'll regret.'

Wynnie backed up a step. Good thing, too, as from nowhere the Sloane guy swung, and connected, and big, bad Dylan Kelly spun on his heel to land square on both feet facing his opponent. His eyes were so dark they were no longer so impossibly blue, a smear of blood appeared on his lower lip, and his right fist was clenched into a white ball.

Instinct be damned, Wynnie threw herself between them. Dylan's eyes connected with hers, and cleared enough that he held himself in check.

She shook her head, still slightly stunned. She knew without a doubt he'd have hit back if he'd had the chance. But there were cameras everywhere. He'd come to her defence, it was her turn to come to his.

She blinked, then ran her thumb across his lip. It came away glistening with his blood, and tingling with the sensation of having done such an intimate thing.

She held it up to him. He frowned, then his tongue darted out and licked at the split in his lip. Then he glanced down at her thumb and before she knew what he was about to do he had the end of her thumb in his mouth as his tongue curled around the tip. Once it was clean, he let her go.

She wrapped her other hand around her thumb the second she had it back, but no manner of squeezing could rid her of the heat radiating from the spot.

Wynnie glanced over her shoulder to find a crowd had gathered, but Sloane was nowhere to be seen. Meaning the coward knew he was in deep trouble. And if they hadn't already, she and Dylan had become the talk of the party.

Things couldn't get any worse for her reputation. She grabbed Dylan by the hand and snuck him through the crowd as fast as she could until she found a neat spot behind a manicured conifer in the courtyard outside where the decadent light didn't touch.

'Are you okay?' Dylan asked, a hand reaching out to cradle her elbow.

'I'm fine. But I'm not the one who just got myself into a round of fisticuffs.'

Dylan's tongue darted out to the now blood-free spot and Wynnie struggled to stop staring. Such beautifully carved lips, so adept at smiling, so built for kissing. Now marred by a swelling bruise created in an effort to protect her, his lips were even more intoxicating.

'What were you thinking back there?' she asked, looking back into his eyes, only to find that out there in the darkness they were an even scarier proposition than those lips.

'Garry Sloane's a cretin.'

'That's not an answer.' He was far too self-aware to fly off the handle for no good reason.

Though what did she know about him really? He was one of the coolest customers she'd ever known. She wasn't sure his own mother would even be able to decipher one of his smiles, a cheek twitch or a rare flinch.

Oh, what she would have given for a key to those expressions. To know if the man she thought he was might be even close to the truth. To know if the way she felt about him was founded on anything but imprudent desire.

'Dylan,' she begged, instantly regretting the longing twinge in her voice nobody would mistake.

The hand at her elbow moved up her arm, sliding the red silk against her overheated skin. 'Believe me, whatever Sloane wanted from you, don't let him have it. I wouldn't wish the guy on my worst enemy.'

Wynnie planted her backside against the mossy concrete planter box, and Dylan's hand fell away. The seat was cold through her dress. She snuck her hands down to grip it all the same. 'Is that how you think of me? As your enemy?'

He kicked the toe of his dress shoe against the concrete,

and his lips curved into a sexy half-smile. 'What makes you think I think of you at all?'

Her heart skittered manically in her chest at the same time that the rest of her grew warm and loose.

She stretched her shoulders back until the muscles in her arms gave her a pleasant kind of hurt. 'If you didn't think of me a little bit it would mean that I'm in the wrong job. And my salary, the corporate headhunters who have me on speed dial and my gut tell me I'm exactly where I should be.'

Shreds of moonlight poked through the tree behind her, picking out his sharp white incisors as his smile grew.

He snuck a hand into his trouser pocket and leant down to her. 'Fine. I think about you plenty. More than I think you'd really like to know. Happy?'

Happy? Not so much happy as tipped upside down and turned inside out.

He grinned, then swore mightily and spun away to press the back of his hand against the split in his lip that he'd just reopened. The split lip he'd endured because of her.

She stood, her silk dress made a horrible sound as it separated from the concrete. It'd be pilled to bits. Thankfully, like every piece of clothing she owned, it was a designer second and had already lived a worthwhile life.

In her high heels her eyes were level with his mouth. His tongue darted out to his lip, and he winced. Again a mix of guilt and desire had her reaching to touch the wound, but this time common sense came to the rescue and her finger stopped short of its mark.

He took her fingers and gently urged her to do as she pleased. Wrapped in his warm grasp, her finger traced the contour of his lip, slowly, carefully, sliding over the bruised bump.

When his hand dropped away, hers continued its path—mapping the indent of his cheek, running over the edge of his sharp jaw, tracing the line where subtle stubble met the smooth skin of his throat, and finishing by sliding into the soft darker hair at the base of his neck.

There she finally came to her senses, her fingers curling into her palm as she pulled it away, but the warmth of his skin and the texture of his wholly masculine roughness were stained onto her tingling fingers for good.

She looked down at her purse as she said, 'Your lip will feel much better much quicker if you get ice onto it as soon as possible.'

'I suppose so. Where would you suggest I find some ice at this time of night?'

She sucked in a deep breath through her nose, ignored the red flag waving madly in the back of her mind and looked him in the eye as she said, 'How does my place sound?'

CHAPTER SEVEN

WYNNIE opened the small cabinet behind the mirror in her bathroom in the hopes she would find something there which might warrant the fact that, rather than asking Dylan's driver to take him to the hospital, she'd brought him home.

After madly text-messaging Hannah, explaining she'd found her own way home, she'd left Dylan sitting in her small lounge room, draped over her rented chocolate leather couch with its so-new-it-still-had-a-tag-attached red angora throw rug, his shirt undone at the collar, his bow tie dangling from his neck, holding his Scotch on ice to his lip.

She drew in a shaky breath. Could a guy seriously be any sexier if he tried? Maybe that was why he was so sexy. He didn't *have* to try. It just oozed from his very pores. And he was sitting in her lounge room…

Eventually she came out of the closet with make-up-remover wipes, antiseptic cream that had travelled with her over three continents and was probably out of date and Band-Aids with butterfly pictures on them, which she'd been a sucker and spent a third more on than the plain ones when she'd done her first Brisbane grocery shop.

She closed the cupboard door and caught her reflection in the mirror. Hair that earlier had been sleek waves was mussed, as if she'd just rolled out of bed. Her hours-old make-up was less than perfect, smudged about her muddy brown eyes making them look huge. And she looked tired. Tired and wired.

Wired because on the interminable town-car ride to her house she'd realised that even though Dylan had arrived at the exact right moment to get her away from Sloane, it wouldn't be long before he came after her again.

Leaving town was one hell of a strong option. Not facing Sloane meant keeping her anonymity, and protecting Felix—wherever he was. But she'd be letting so many people down. She'd not get the chance to continue rekindling the only real adult friendship she'd ever had or to experience a Brisbane summer after so many winters in Europe. It all felt like a cruel joke.

Not to mention the fact that she'd be walking away from the man currently pacing around her small lounge room. The man who'd leapt to her defence without thought of what it might cost him.

She heard a noise from outside the bathroom, and flinched. Had the noise been a door shutting? Had he gone? No. There was music. He'd found her miserably small CD collection in a drawer of her coffee table. Sting crooned from her rented speakers.

Out there making himself at home was a man brimming with power, self-esteem, brutal sexual energy. She wanted so badly to know what he tasted like, her own lips tasted sweet and salty.

She wasn't going anywhere. Not tonight anyway.

'What the hell am I thinking?' she begged of her reflection.

It practically smirked back at her. She'd brought this on herself. She'd flirted, and pushed, and prodded and made herself a part of his world, so that he had no chance but to notice her above and beyond the hundred odd fresh-faced souls who begged him for face time each and every day. And now he'd noticed her, all right. Now she had every chance of getting up close and personal.

But she wouldn't count her chickens. This might turn out to all be blissfully innocent. She might patch him up, then he might happily go on his way. And a pig might fly into her lounge room and offer to make them both cups of chamomile tea.

'No time like the present to find out,' she said. Then ducked her head, grabbed her medicinal paraphernalia, took a deep breath and opened the bathroom door.

Dylan sat on Wynnie's couch, downing the last of his Scotch as he waited for her to return from wherever it was she'd been hiding.

His eyes glanced over blonde-wood floors, windows looking out over a lush backyard, lashings of moonlight spilling inside creating silver swatches on the floor, and fat gold beeswax candles burning discreetly on a bunch of surfaces.

As far as he could tell there was not another light on in the house. If he didn't know her as well as he already did he might have thought this a scene fit for seduction rather than frugal energy use. As it was, it only made him smile.

The woman might have enough darkness in her past to need to go by an alias, but at least she was no hypocrite.

He stared into the melting ice in his glass and frowned. Why did *that* suddenly feel like an important discovery considering the mound of concrete, black-and-white evidence he'd collected on her already?

Just as Dylan was about to call in a search party, Wynnie reappeared.

She'd changed from her slinky red dress, half the reason he hadn't been able to keep his damn eyes and hands and thoughts off her all night, into loose grey track pants and an even more shapeless red sweatshirt. She'd discarded the sexy high heels in lieu of bare feet.

He bit back a grin. She was so obviously trying her dandiest to appear asexual, but it just wasn't working. Little did she know the pants clung to the curve of her buttocks as she walked, and that the red sweater had slipped off her right shoulder just enough that he could see the edge of a white lace

)ra strap. The hint of what lay beneath was even sexier than he blatant, smack down, luscious, clingy number that had had him in such a state all night long.

'Nice place you've got here,' he said.

'It belongs to the CFC—they're letting me stay here for the meantime. It was built green. Solar panels, shaded windows, double-glazed glass and the like.'

'Candles included?'

In the silver light of the moon he could still tell her cheeks had pinked. 'They're all mine.'

'Oh, and your phone beeped while you were in there,' Dylan said as she knelt on the other side of the coffee table.

Her golden eyes shot to his. 'Did you check it?'

He laughed, then sat forward, cradling his still-throbbing mouth. 'What kind of man do you think I am?'

'I'm sure I have no idea.'

She laid out a strange collection of wares on the coffee table. His bruise gave a sharp little pulse as he realised she wasn't as pedantically organised domestically as she was professionally—another insignificant snippet that felt as if it held more weight than it ought to have when compared with Jack's discoveries.

He poked his finger at a Band-Aid with a pink butterfly upon it. 'Suddenly I feel a desperate need to know what kind of men you usually bring back to your place to… soothe.'

She afforded him a blank stare. 'Alas your need will remain unassuaged.'

He could have taken that line so many ways. The minx. He laughed again, his lip hurt more, and this time it was followed by a pretty rambunctious oath. 'Jeez, woman. Stop making me laugh and heal me.'

He left his now-watery Scotch behind and lay back on the couch, one leg resting on the seat, the other foot still connected to the floor, his far arm tucked behind his head.

She cleared her throat, a small pucker formed between he
brows, telling him at least she planned on trying to do a good
job of nursemaid.

Her teeth began tugging at her bottom lip leaving in thei
wake a sheen that turned his whole body to stone.

'Relax,' she insisted, her voice anything but. 'I'll be witl
you in just a sec.'

He closed his eyes and tried to do as he was told.

Not as though that was in any way why he was there. Or why
she had invited him there. Meaning they were both unhinged

Now he knew without a doubt that she had agendas above
and beyond those she espoused, he ought to have washed hi:
hands of her for good—Wynnie Devereaux, or Guinevere
Lambert or whoever she was.

And then bloody Garry Sloane had oozed up from the gut-
ter and pounced.

The second he'd overheard that bastard of all the possible
bastards call her by her real name, his instinct had sent him
flying in there like a frenzied whirlwind.

True, he'd hired Jack to uncover the skeletons in her closet
in case *he* might one day need to use them to protect his own
interests. No altruism at all, pure self-protection. That was
why he *should* have swept her away from Sloane.

But watching her standing there, panic and pain lighting
her eyes as her past was about to be spilled on the floor at her
feet, he'd imagined how it would feel if someone like Sloane
stumbled upon the truth of his father's failing health, how
exposing that news would hurt his family, how it would cut
him to the bone…

Blinded by completely soft-headed empathy, he had only
been able to think of saving Wynnie from that kind of hurt.

He blamed those eyes, those damned, compassionate, big,
liquid-brown eyes. It seemed in searching for her Achilles'
heel, he'd only ended up exposing his own.

A wave of warmth washed over him, followed by the gentle draw of her floral scent. He opened one eye to find her leaning over him.

She squeezed a big gloop of cream onto an oversized cotton swab-like thing, and Dylan wondered if he ought to ask for a spoon to bite down on before she got any closer.

'So how did you end up working for the CFC?' he asked.

The swab hovered. She'd refused to answer a similar question before. But something made her change her mind. 'My friend Hannah, you met her tonight, she works for their legal department. They needed a campaign. A new image. She begged me to head it up. I loved the concept to bits. I couldn't say no.'

'Why would you have wanted to?'

She sat back on her haunches and her eyes shot to his. Now he knew where her vulnerability and motivation both sprang from, the caution that masked every word out of her mouth was as clear as day.

'I enjoy living abroad.' She reached out to him, dabbing at his lip, and the cold of the cream actually felt nice.

'Verona, right?' he said between dabs.

She tensed, and pressed slightly too hard against his lip. He flinched and so did she. 'You've asked around about me?'

He bit his tongue. 'Someone mentioned it in passing. Something to do with encouraging the good folk thereabouts to give generously to help renovate the Arena. Wasn't it once a colosseum? All lions and gladiators battling to the death? Not the kind of place I would imagine a big softie like you getting all het up about.'

'Every inch of this planet has at one time or another been a place of bloodshed and bad decisions. The nice part about being enlightened is that we can hopefully learn from our mistakes and aim to do better.'

His chest rumbled with laughter. 'Now if that isn't a stump speech you've said a hundred times before, I don't know what is. I can't believe you're trying to sell your proposal to me now, while I'm lying here bleeding.'

'You're not bleeding,' she scoffed, not denying his accu-sation. 'I'm actually beginning to wonder if he hit you at all or if you just got a fright and bit your lip.'

He laughed all the harder and his lip stung so much he licked it to taste blood. He glared at her, to find her biting her own lip to stop from laughing.

'Anyway, you brought it up,' she said, 'and it's not like your every waking minute isn't taken up with finding ways to make people believe that putting their faith in KInG is all they'll ever need.'

He licked his lip again and realised her gauze was just waving in the breeze as her eyes were locked on his lip, his tongue. He gave his lip one last swipe, her eyes following it precisely, before putting it away. He wondered if she had any clue how many waking minutes over the past days had been dedicated entirely to her.

He pushed himself up on his elbow. 'So if you don't own this place, where do you have your money invested?'

'Oh, no,' she said waggling a finger at him. 'You are not going to sell me on investing with KInG.'

'There are no rules with what you and I are doing, Wynnie. That's the fun part—we get to make it up as we go along.'

She blinked, weighing his words. 'Fine. My money's in the bank.'

'Putting all your eggs in one basket is never a smart thing to do. To protect yourself, you need to hedge your invest-ments. Diversify.'

She glanced at him from beneath her lashes and grew very still. He searched her eyes, looking for clues as to what she was thinking now that he had more pieces of the puzzle.

But all he got was the distinct feeling that she had already figured him out long before he came close to figuring her out. That she might actually be wondering how soon he might need to 'diversify' if anything actually happened between the two of them.

'Stop talking and lie down or we'll never get you out of here,' she said, pressing his chest until he did as he was told.

But as he gazed into her hot honey eyes he knew, once and for all, that there was no 'if' about it. The only question was when.

She tucked a swathe of her mussed dark hair behind her ear, and her brow tightened in concentration as she sat up on her knees and gingerly angled some kind of cold, wet bandage over his lip, her stomach pressing into his free arm as she twisted, the lower part of her breasts sliding over his ribcage as she twisted again.

Seriously, how was a man to bear it?

Wynnie patted Dylan's lip as gingerly as she could. It wasn't as though she had a single clue if what she was doing was really helping, but he wasn't complaining, or telling her she was doing it wrong, so she must have been doing something right.

The wound wasn't as bad as it had first seemed. Some swelling, which the iced drink had taken down. And she was fairly sure a bruise would arrive through the night. But it, thankfully, didn't require a butterfly Band-Aid.

Tending it, on the other hand, was sweet agony.

His clean scent, his hard body reposed beneath her, and those lips tugging beneath her gentle fingers. If she ever truly required punishment for mistakes of her past, then this was it—the impossibility of wanting Dylan Kelly and the enduring ache it left in the region of her heart.

She shot to her feet, the fresh air swarming between them allowing her to catch her breath.

Then his hand wrapped about her ankle. She got such a fright she dropped everything in her hands. Make-up wipes floated to her floor like snow.

'Dylan,' she warned, her voice husky.

'Wynnie,' he returned, in a voice she'd never heard before. It was so deep, so dark, so blatantly hungry she actually shivered.

'What are you doing?' she asked.

His cheek lifted. His hand slid further up her calf, sliding the wide hem of her track pants with it. 'What do you think I'm doing?'

Something you shouldn't, she thought before her eyes drifted closed and she breathed out hard through her nose.

Accidental touches, touches under the guise of being polite or professional—to this moment that had been it. And each and every one of those innocuous touches had set her nerves alight. His purposeful touch was irresistible.

'What are you doing all the way over there?' he asked, giving her a tug and putting her off balance.

'I'm done,' she said. 'You're on your way to being healed.'

'Honey, we're not even close to done.' He sat up, slowly, his eyes not leaving hers, his hand sliding up her leg till it rested on her outer thigh, holding her in place. 'Tell me why you brought me here?'

'To fix your war wounds. You stood up for me and I felt beholden. I always pay my debts.'

Dylan just laughed, the sound trembling down her thighs into the backs of her knees. He tugged, she twisted and she was beside him on the couch.

'You don't owe me a thing.' He reached up to sink a hand into the hair at the back of her neck. 'And you brought me here because this has been inevitable.'

'What?' she asked, the word barely making it past her lips.

'This.'

He pulled her to him, his lips sliding over hers, a perfect fit, as though they'd been there a thousand times before.

Every other sensation bombarding her, on the other hand, felt entirely new. The way her whole body melted against him like a fire had been lit beneath her. The need to wrap her arms tight about him so that she could be as close as she could possibly be. The build-up of relieved tears behind her eyes.

Then she remembered his split lip. She pulled away as

quickly as she could, which was embarrassingly sluggish. Her finger hovered above his lip. 'Doesn't it hurt?'

'Not a damn bit.'

He sank his face into her neck—it lost all bone structure and fell back to give him all the access he would possibly need.

'You taste like heaven,' he murmured near enough to her ear lobe that she shuddered deliciously.

'Say that again,' she begged.

She could feel his smile against her neck. And this time as he said the words his breath deliberately teased her ear and she let out a groan she could no longer suppress.

He slid her sweatshirt over her head. She tore so furiously at the front of his shirt several buttons popped right off. The sound of them hitting the polished wood floor felt like pebbles pelted hard against the inside of her head.

She let go of his shirt, and sat back with her hand over her mouth. 'Oh, God, I'm so sorry! I broke your shirt.'

He didn't even look to check; his eyes remained locked on hers. 'Not to worry. I have more.'

Of course he did, but that wasn't what had psyched her out. Her own wild abandon, the effortless loss of control—how deep could those untapped dimensions of herself possibly go?

In the resultant silence, she realised she wasn't the only one who was caught in the deep end. Dylan's breaths came thick and fast. The tendons in his neck stood out as if the blood flowed through his body at twice its normal rate. His eyes were so dark she wouldn't have known their true colour if it weren't permanently etched on her mind.

Her hand dropped from her mouth to grab the edge of the couch cushion for balance. Strands of her hair were stuck to her neck with sweat. Her heart rate was frantic. Her legs were wrapped about his hips and from the waist up she wore nothing but a delicate lace bra.

But she might as well have been naked for the way the look in his eyes made her feel. There was nowhere left to hide. Not behind her job, her name, her past. And for the first time in her life she felt herself living, right smack bang in the middle of the moment.

And then he slowly undid the rest of his buttons, and slid his jacket and shirt from his back.

Her eyes roved hungrily over his chest. His tanned skin was sculpted, smooth and perfect. The arrow of dark blond hair beginning at his navel and disappearing into his black trousers made her mouth turn completely dry.

No one human being had the right to look the way he looked. And she knew he was no angel. The fact that her skin felt hot, and slippery, as if it were tugging from her body, certainly assured her of that.

But now she had the taste of him in her mouth, the scent of him in her nose, on her clothes, constantly wafting across the back of her mind, reason took a backseat.

He reached out, his hands sliding around her waist, and he pulled her more fully into his lap. What little breath remained in her lungs left in a heady whoosh.

'No regrets,' he said, his voice rough.

She shook her head. She wouldn't be sorry for this. It was inevitable. It was chemical. It was nature's intent. And who was she, a hippy child from Nimbin, to argue with nature?

Wynnie slid her hands over his shoulders, the heat and curve of hard muscle giving her strength. She let temptation continue to guide her as her fingers delved into the short thick hair at the back of his neck. It fluttered through her fingers like velvet.

Then she leant in and kissed him. Open mouth. Tongue. Eyes closed. Luscious. Wet. Decadent.

He groaned into her mouth as he wrapped his arms so tightly around her she could barely breathe. But she didn't care. All she needed was his hot skin, his undisciplined grip.

Only this time she really let go, and just let whatever would happen happen.

Every sensation heightened. Every touch, every shift of skin on skin, every catch of breath, every aching groan, every tantalising breath that whispered across her neck, her ear, the swell of her breasts, her hot lips. She imagined this must be what it felt like to be high.

Dylan Kelly was her drug of choice. And, despite the pleasure bombarding her from every angle, she knew he was the most dangerous kind of addiction she would ever know.

His hands moved to the clasp of her bra, unlocking it with practised finesse. He'd done it before. Many times if rumours were to be believed.

She closed her eyes tight to shut out the thread of doubt that brought on. The extent of his experience was the only hope she had that they'd be able to find a way to be professional after they were through.

Slowly, deliberately, his thumbs traced the outline of each and every rib as though it was something he'd fantasised about doing. His fingers slid around her sides to press firmly into the always tight muscles below her shoulder blades causing her to arch towards him.

Then his mouth moved to her breast, his breath washing across the taut peak sweeping every thought from her mind but pleasure. She cried out her thanks and arched closer.

The feather-light touch of his tongue circling her nipple was too much. But then it was nothing compared with the heat that rocketed through her body as he took her breast in his mouth.

She bit her lip to stop from crying out that he take her then and there. Because no matter how great the ache, it was an ache she found herself imagining she could live with for the rest of her life.

His teeth scraped painfully around her breast before pulling away. The cooling night air tickled at the moist spot and she broke out in an array of goose bumps.

His brow furrowed, and then he set to righting the wrong, his hands again running over every exposed inch of her.

'Your skin,' he rumbled. 'It's like fresh butter. I've never in my life felt anything so soft.'

He slid from the couch and sank to his knees before her. Then he leant in and ran his tongue along the curve of her lowest rib. She breathed in deep as it curled into her navel and along the top of her track pants. He nudged them downwards so that he could scrape his teeth gently along her hip bone. She wasn't sure whose moan was louder.

'God,' he groaned, running his thumb along the smooth skin an inch below her hip bone, 'could you possibly taste any better?'

'Caramel tart,' she said on a sigh. 'Tonight at the ball, there was a spare seat next to mine. I had seconds. By now it's probably leeching through my skin.'

His laughter reverberated through her bottom half. The delectable shudder that followed was worth it.

His breath whispered against the rise of her belly as he said, 'Mmm. I'm not sure that's it. I have the distinct feeling the taste I can't get enough of is all you.'

Using the finger stroking her hip, he tugged at her track pants and her bottom shifted lower on the couch. Another tug and they were gone, leaving her naked in the moonlight, bar a nude, seamless, barely there G-string tiny enough not to have shown under her silk dress.

Before she had the chance to even wonder about her bikini line, the G-string was gone—sliding down her legs, scraping delectably along her calves, and over her feet, and gone. Flicked away. Hanging from a palm frond in the corner of the room.

If she hadn't known she was in the middle of the most decadent night of her young life, that clinched it.

Her eyes were drawn back to his. And it was only then that she realised he was still covered from the waist down, and thus, to all intents and purposes, dressed.

Her knees pressed together and she pulled herself into a more dignified upright position. 'Somehow the balance of power has gone all your way,' she said.

'Wynnie, my sweet, you have got that all wrong.' His eyes roved over her body, adoring it, worshipping it as he said, 'You have me in your complete thrall.'

She crossed her legs, and crossed her arms. 'So if I brought out a certain contract and waved it before your nose...'

His eyes turned so dark she thought she might have pushed her luck a centimetre too far. Until he grinned like a shark and lay his hands upon her knees, drawing them back apart. 'How could I hope to hold a pen when my hands are so pleasantly occupied otherwise?'

How indeed.

Ignoring her round-about request that he disrobe, he instead returned to focus on her. He caressed her right leg, from her knee to her toes, massaging, melting. Then when he had her completely boneless he lifted her leg and lay it atop his shoulder.

The pure audacity sapped her breath from her lungs and her wide eyes shot straight to his. He smiled, and waited. Making sure she was okay.

She wasn't exactly sure how to tell him she was more than okay, bar smiling back. Her cheeks felt shaky, her lips swollen and halfway numb. But it was obviously enough.

His mouth hovered at the juncture between her legs. It took every ounce of strength she had not to delve her fingers into his hair to guide him.

He looked up, and his eyes pierced hers. 'Now tell me why you really brought me here.'

She slapped a hand over her eyes and bit back a scream. 'Are you truly going to make me say it?'

'I'm the devil, remember. It's par for the course.'

She licked her lips as his breath washed across her thighs. 'Fine,' she croaked. 'I brought you here because I wanted this. All of this. From the second you came strolling through that crowd outside your great big phallus of a building and saw me handcuffed to your statue like dinner waiting for you on a plate, I wanted you.'

And any other words she might have had in store were lost in a groan as he lowered his head.

Her arms shot out and her hands gripped the back of the couch. Her eyes slammed closed and her head snapped back.

His absolute tenderness astounded her. His deftness did not. It met her expectations and then steadily blew them out of the water.

Sweet agony lapped at her core. Wave after hot, liquid wave swelled and surged until she no longer had any control of her mind, or her body.

'I can't do this.'

'You can,' he murmured, kissing one thigh, then the other, letting her come down off the crest of the wave just long enough to catch her breath before taking her higher still.

Her skin prickled with sweat, her fingers grew numb from hanging on so tight, and every nerve felt aflame as the pressure inside her built to a beautiful crescendo.

And on and on it went. Higher, harder, deeper, bliss. Building still until she was sure she would faint from the violence of the pleasure rising inside her.

And just when she thought she couldn't take it any more numbness overcame her, the eye of the storm giving her respite, making her feel as if she were floating above the couch.

Then pleasure as she had never known crashed over her, and she shattered into a thousand hot, dark, beautiful pieces.

Cruel as he was, Dylan didn't even give her a chance to live out the waves cascading over her. He kissed her thigh, stroked her hip, ran his tongue up her waist and the edge of her left breast. It was torture, pure and simple.

He ran his hands along her arms, uncurling her fingers from their death grip of the rug-covered leather, and slowly lay her back on the couch.

Replete, boneless, weak, she stretched her arms over her head and twisted her body back into a more normal shape.

Dylan, now standing over her, watched her with his hand

on his fly. 'Why do I get the feeling you have no idea how beautiful you are?'

Wynnie curled onto her side, still warm and buzzing. 'Flattery will get you everywhere.'

'Maybe so, but I've never found cause to use it.' He pulled down his zip, then after that his trousers, until he stood before her—naked, ready and godlike.

Silver moonlight caressed his muscled form as though it had merely been waiting for the chance to do so. Every dip and depression seemed caved from marble. Every curve and rise all man.

He was right. He'd never need to use flattery to get what he wanted. He just had to ask.

She pushed herself up on one arm and held out her other hand. He knelt over her. She wrapped her arms about his torso, arching into him as he pressed her back on the couch. And their kiss was like nothing she had ever known.

Heat exploded through her body, spot fires sprang up all over her skin. She wanted him so badly, but even though she could feel the tension in his arms, in his legs, in his kiss, he still spent every second making sure her pleasure was paramount.

Sweeping her damp hair from her face. Tugging at her bottom lip, which made her moan every time. Sliding his free hand down her side, teasing, lightly caressing the outside of her breast when she wanted his whole hand thereon. Brushing her hip bone with his knuckles with a whisper-light touch that had her arching higher towards him, wanting more. Then from nowhere sinking his fingers deep between her legs, drawing her back to the brink of destruction again and again.

Need and desire were the only two things keeping them on that couch. The fact that he had a condom on hand now felt like a miracle, as well.

He sheathed himself. She wrapped her legs around him. And finally he sank into her with a shuddering sigh.

He filled her and then some, stretching every part of her

until she felt more, on every level there was, than she'd ever felt before.

Her breath came in gasps. Her fingers dug into his back. Beauty and exhilaration overcame her. Time expanded and compressed as her world shrank to the size of her couch as she rocked with him, pressed into him, enveloped him, took of him everything he had.

With the brakes off it felt as if they were careening down a steep hill. She could barely breathe; she could barely think. It was terrifying and exhilarating and she didn't want it to end.

And then the rhythm changed, hastened. Power surged through her, giving her the knowledge that it was her turn to bring him release.

She looked deep into his eyes, the deepest ocean blue, and he looked right on back as together they reached the highest heights before sliding into oblivion.

And as she fought her way back into consciousness Wynnie felt the heart whose life force had long since been compartmentalised to care for greater causes, the heart she had been sure would never truly be touched again, make a hot, heavy return to life.

CHAPTER EIGHT

As Dylan sat upon the overly soft green couch on the set of the Sunday-morning chat show, eyes closed tight as his face was powdered, he tried his very best to concentrate on what he had to say over the next ten minutes, and not on Wynnie as he'd left her less than eight hours earlier.

Standing in the doorway of her home, a short satin robe barely wrapped about her deliciously naked body, her bare legs twisted together, her dark hair cascading over her slender shoulders, her hand wrapped loosely around the doorframe as she leant up to kiss him goodnight.

It had all been so civilised. As civilised as he'd ever known it to be. So why then did he feel more like a tightly coiled spring than he had before releasing every ounce of energy he had inside him with the best sex of his life?

'Dylan!'

He blinked and the bright lights of the TV studio came back into focus to find Rylie Madigan, the anchor of *Daybreak*, and one of his sister's best friends, slapping him across the upper arm.

'Where the hell are you?' she whispered between her perfectly capped teeth.

He thought cooling thoughts, flapped his suit jacket and repositioned himself on the over-soft couch. Through gritted teeth he said, 'Same place I am every Sunday morning, my backside parked on this exact spot as I prepare to pass out the good investment word to your loyal viewers across this fair land.'

Rylie tilted her chin so her long blonde hair could be fluffed and coiffed. 'Sweet cheeks, don't go acting like you are here out of the goodness of your heart. I should be getting a finder's fee for the mum-and-dad clients who flock to your business because I let you and your pretty face charm the sense out of them on my show.'

Dylan grunted. She was right. He never did anything unless it served the family's interests.

So why then had he gone and slept with the woman who was doing her everything to make them all seem like avaricious jerks? Why? Because he was a man not nearly as in control of his hormones as he'd always thought he was, that was for bloody sure.

He reached out and pinched Rylie's cheek. 'The fact that you don't even think about trying to take advantage of us like that is the reason we let Meg keep you around.'

'Nice. Oh, and did my producers tell you they found a super-fun way to mix things up a bit today?' Rylie's green gaze slid past his shoulder. Something in her smile put his muddied instincts back on high alert. He tensed and turned.

And as if he'd dreamt her up out of the most wretched, disobedient, self-flagellating depths inside him, Wynnie Devereaux stood in the wings shaking hands with the producers, hand to her heart, smiling, flirting, winning them over as easily as she won over every poor soul who stood in her path.

A young guy in jeans, T-shirt and headphones tapped her on the shoulder and pointed to the soft, fat couches on which he and Rylie sat.

She squinted in their direction, saw him there and nodded. He offered a subtle bow in response. If he wanted to know how civilised things could truly be, this set-up would show him.

She touched each cohort on the arm as she took her leave,

then lifted her high-heel-shod feet as she skipped over the thick electrical cords gaffer-taped to the floor.

Dressed in a blousy cream top, a cream skirt hugging her curves to just below her knees, a loose bronze belt skimming her hips, with her hair loose and soft, she looked like an angel, meaning in comparison in his dark grey suit, sharp white shirt and red tie he'd look like the poster boy for corporate greed.

And the closer Wynnie got, the clearer it all became. The outfit, the lack of surprise in her eyes—she had to have known she was coming here today. And all the night before, as they'd danced, as he'd come to her rescue, as she'd played nurse-maid, as they'd come together naked, she *had* to have known he was going to be here, too.

And she'd never once mentioned a thing.

He uncrossed his legs and dug his fingers into his thighs. The marks they would leave would be nothing on the red weals across his back from where her fingernails had dug into him as she had climaxed in his arms.

He allowed himself, and her, a break. Maybe this had been a last-minute arrangement. Maybe she'd only found out about it that morning. Maybe in the heat of the moment it had simply been forgotten.

Or maybe she'd unscrupulously taken him for the great cuckold he seemed determined to prove he could be.

'You all right, hon?' Rylie asked from somewhere to his left. 'You look like you've seen a ghost.'

Wynnie hit the patch of hot light beaming down upon the small stage, caught his eye and smiled. Cool, calm, confident, with not a lick of vulnerability to be seen.

'No ghost,' Dylan said. But certainly a tunnel of light.

Wynnie sashayed past Dylan and made herself known to the host of the show.

At least she hoped she'd sashayed.

From the moment she'd clapped eyes on him, lounging in

the couch, cool as you please, right at home under the glaring down lights, nothing about him registering the wildly intimate night they'd shared the night before, her feet had felt like lead, her knees as if mini earthquakes were erupting beneath her kneecaps with every step, and her clothes felt as if she'd put them on backwards.

She'd known he'd be here. It was in the brief the producers had faxed to her that morning, which she'd read in the cab on the way to the row of TV stations atop Mt Coot-tha.

If she'd known he'd be there before she was halfway up the mountain? If she'd known the nerveless reaction she was going to get? For the first time in her career she probably would have feigned the mumps.

'So glad you could come,' Rylie Madigan said with a grin, and Wynnie was glad for the change of focus. 'Nothing like fresh blood to shake up a comfortable old city like ours.'

'Happy to oblige.'

'I read a bit about you in the papers over the past few days. I'd love to take you to lunch sometime to pick your brain about a few things.'

Rylie glanced at Dylan. Wynnie felt as if she was missing something.

Dylan grabbed his glass of water, took his time sipping, then placed it on the coffee table and stood, stretching his arms over his head, and said, 'Say yes, Ms Devereaux, she's not hitting on you.'

Wynnie's cheeks pinked in an instant, less from the sexy rumble of his voice, and much more from the unduly cool Ms Devereaux remark. 'I didn't… Of course I…'

Rylie laughed. 'Ignore him. He's a fiend. He takes his greatest pleasure from winding women up and watching them spin away as fast as possible. The lovely Lilliana's fault right there. That's what a succubus for an ex-fiancée will do to a guy.'

A succubus? *And* an ex-fiancée? Wynnie silently fumed as these new snippets sank in. Hannah needed a good talking to about timely revelation of important information. And her researchers were going to have a little meeting with her all on their own.

She couldn't help herself; she looked to Dylan again. He seemed not to have heard a thing, but she saw his fingers curl into his palm. She knew that feeling—clenching was the only way you could keep the bad things locked up tight inside.

Her first instinct was to soothe his pain. Again. But there was nothing in his bearing to give her any indication that she now had that right. She wasn't his girlfriend. She wasn't even really a friend. She was barely a prospective business associate.

'So, lunch?' Rylie asked. 'We'll get Meg to come, too. She's out there in the audience somewhere, playing her portable PlayStation thingie while she waits for me to finish. It'll be a riot.'

'Sure. That'd be lovely. Call my office and we'll make a time.'

Rylie's brow then furrowed, her lips turned down and Wynnie got the feeling she was doing her best impression of solemn. 'Now, back to our regular programming. I know that your agenda is a serious one. Saving the planet and all that. Go you! But remember we're a super-relaxed show. Our viewers aren't tuning in for anything hard-hitting or ultra-political. So best thing is to keep it light.'

'Can do,' Wynnie said as brightly as she could while her stomach felt as if it were trying to digest a pound of lead.

Rylie grinned, and somehow didn't wrinkle, then moved Wynnie to a soft couch on the other side of the stage from Dylan's.

She sat, crossed her legs, and suddenly the floor manager was flapping a two-minute signal, and the eyes of the cameras grew large as they zoomed in close. Wynnie's heart rate made itself known as adrenalin surged through her body.

Though the last thing she needed two minutes before a live TV interview was adrenaline on top of her adrenaline, she shifted her gaze a fraction until she found a pair of daring blue eyes.

The night before those eyes had roved over every inch of her naked skin, drinking her in as though he were quenching a lifetime of thirst. But now the level of indifference he was maintaining even as their eyes held for second after second made her body clench from top to toe.

She wasn't his girlfriend. She wasn't a friend. And the harsh truth that was finally dawning on her was that she wasn't even really his lover.

She'd been warned, more than once, and she'd known it deep down inside all along. But she'd blithely ignored it until the truth slapped her hard across the face.

She'd said it herself. Dylan was a flirt. The art was his greatest weapon.

In their game the sell was not nearly as much about showcasing the high points of a product itself as much as it was about creating a blissful buying experience. It was their job to be memorable, delicious and addictive. To make sure that even while they were shaking their head 'no' a prospective client was thinking ahead to when they might come back for more.

Looking into his cool dark eyes, she wondered *how* she'd let herself go so long without remembering that.

'Today we have something special for you,' Rylie's singsong voice rang out and Wynnie realised they were on.

She blinked, found a smile, found a camera and found her centre. She'd sort the other stuff out later, when there weren't hundreds of thousands of people looking in.

Rylie continued, 'Not only do we have our regular financial advisor, Dylan Kelly, head of Media Relations for the Kelly Investment Group, we also have Wynnie Devereaux, a representative for the Clean Footprint Coalition who has come along with some advice of her own. Welcome to the both of you.'

Dylan smiled for the people, and even Wynnie, who knew better, had flutters in her stomach at the flirtatious light in his eyes. When he turned that light her way, her heart tumbled, twisted, second-guessed itself and then went back to pumping blood and left confusion to take over her head instead.

She blinked, then somehow beamed at Rylie. 'Thanks for having me, Rylie.'

Rylie leant forward, draping her manicured hands over her knees. 'Now, is it true that you first met our Dylan when you handcuffed yourself to a statue outside his building?'

Wynnie laughed to cover the fact that she was barely registering Rylie's words. 'I'm afraid it takes more than a polite phone call to get the attention of a representative of a big firm like KInG. And considering the changes I believe they could make in order to help reduce energy consumption in this city are beyond compare, this girl had to do what a girl had to do.'

The small studio audience cheered. She just knew any woman at home watching would be cheering, too. Putting themselves in her shoes, imagining the day they might find reason for a showdown with a man like Dylan.

She glanced at the man in question to find he certainly did not look in the mood to cheer. If the women at home knew the havoc a showdown with such a man wrought, they might change their minds.

Rylie's sharp gaze swung to him and Wynnie drew in a deep breath. 'Did you really refuse to return Wynnie's phone calls? How could you? She's adorable!'

Dylan's returning smile was beautiful enough for the people at home, but Wynnie knew he was struggling not to throttle Rylie, their good host.

'Yeah,' Wynnie threw in, to all of their amazement. 'How adorable does a businesswoman with a great idea have to be to get the great and wonderful Dylan Kelly to call her back?'

His gaze slid to hers—hot, dark, menacing. Warning her to back down. But she had to take out her frustration on somebody, and he was so perfectly positioned to bear the brunt.

He shuffled forward on his seat, seemingly not the least

bit intimidated by the dual front. And then his eyes locked back onto hers.

'Ms Devereaux,' he said, his voice as smooth and hot as melting wax, 'being that you are so new in town, perhaps you didn't realise that we are a financial institution whose job it is to look out for the interests of our clients. If you had an investment query, I'd be happy to take a meeting with you. Any time.'

Wynnie licked her dry lips. She wondered if anyone else thought that by *'meeting'* he meant hot, sweaty, naked, sex. Any time. By the twitters and sighs pouring from the studio audience she figured they probably did. She only wished she knew if his offer was good, or just for the cameras.

'Mr Kelly,' she said, her voice huskier than she would have liked, but now she'd gone down this road she couldn't turn back. 'Book me a room, and I'll be there.'

It took a few moments of dead air, but then Dylan smiled. 'I might just do that.'

It was the first real smile she'd had from him since she'd walked into the studio. It was beautiful, breathtaking, real, and all for her.

She smiled right on back. In fact, she had to bite her tongue to stop from laughing out loud. Somehow it eased her tension and ramped it up all at the same time. She only hoped the sudden heat in her cheeks was lost in the wash of hard white light.

'My one good deed for the day,' Rylie said, and then Wynnie remembered where she was.

'No good deed goes unpunished,' Dylan warned, plainly having never forgotten for a second that he was on show.

Rylie looked down the barrel of the camera as she said, 'Now, my lovelies, let's go through Wynnie's list of ways we can each and every one of us reduce our energy consumption and save money at the same time, then Dylan can give us some advice on how to start saving now for Christmas.'

She glanced at Wynnie, then at Dylan, waggling her

long fingers at the two of them. 'Now who could have possibly guessed that your interests would converge so beautifully as all that?'

'Not this little duck,' Dylan said.

Wynnie somehow bit out a smile.

And Rylie's eyes gleamed as bullet points of Wynnie's list came up on the screen.

Fifteen minutes later, Wynnie sat in the green room, waiting for the producer to come by so she could press some flesh, and thank him for the spot.

The door bumped on its hinges, and her heart rate kicked up a notch, hoping instead it might be Dylan. The last thing she wanted was a 'we have to talk' talk, but some kind of clarity was only fair.

The door swung open and closed and a petite brunette, wearing the kind of cute chocolate-brown cocktail dress not usually seen on a person so early on a Sunday morning, slumped onto the couch next to her.

'Hi,' she said, 'I'm Meg.'

Meg Kelly. She hadn't even needed to drop her surname. Her blue eyes were the same as her brother's—bright, mischievous, and, if you looked harder, guarded. But unlike him she was also obviously as sweet as pie.

'I'm waiting to take Rylie out to brunch,' Meg said, 'but I had to pop back here to tell you how much fun that interview was. I've never seen anyone get to my brother like that.'

'Is he around somewhere do you know?' Wynnie slipped in.

'God, no. He snuck out a back exit before the floor manager had barely yelled "clear".'

Wynnie slumped back into her chair.

Meg continued unabated, 'I thought he was about to pop a vein when you said only eight KInG employees out of eight hundred actually car pool to work. You are my new favourite person in the whole world.'

'I don't think I've ever been commended for causing vein popping in anyone before. Maybe a new line for my résumé?'

Meg laughed and held up a fist. 'Rock the establishment!'

Of course Wynnie liked her, and so instantly she almost allowed herself to ask about the succubus ex-fiancée. To find out if he still had feelings for the woman and that was why he was so reticent. To ask if she perhaps knew of a magic pill she could take that would make her forget all about the Kellys forever.

Meg lay a hand on her knee. 'Now, the other reason I'm here is that my parents are having a little get-together at the house this afternoon, just family and a couple of friends, and I'd really love it if you could come.'

It took Wynnie a moment to compute what Meg had just said. 'Oh, no, no, no. If you were really paying attention to that interview you'd know that there is no love lost between your brother and me.'

Her choice of words rang a bell deep inside her, which she thought it best to ignore.

She continued, 'If I set foot on your family's property he would have me shot for trespassing.'

'Rubbish. He's a Labrador. All bark. So you'll come as my guest. Would it help if you knew my reasons were purely selfish? Having the family not entirely focused on why I am not the vice president of some fabulous company like the rest of them are would be nice.'

Meg certainly had the same charisma as her brother; Wynnie could feel it tugging her to do things she oughtn't to want to do. But she shook her head. 'It's very sweet of you to ask, but I just can't.'

Meg sat back, adorably vanquished. She lifted her feet off the floor and seemed to find her bright purple toenails fascinating for several long moments before she said, 'He was talking about you, you know?'

Wynnie slid her butterfly clip from her top, needing something to occupy her while she reeled from having the second female close to Dylan pick up on vibes between them.

'I'm sure my name has been used in vain in the hallowed halls of KInG many a time over the past week.'

Meg dropped her feet, then looked Wynnie square in the eye. 'Maybe so, but I don't hang out at the family biz so I wouldn't know about any of that. This was at a family dinner. He kept bringing the conversation right back to you.'

Wynnie blew warm air on her butterfly and polished it on her skirt.

She said, 'That's what a woman in handcuffs will do to a conversation, I'm afraid.'

But her heart raced. Her mind whirled. And her imagination ran away with itself. Maybe she'd been thinking about this all wrong. Maybe what had happened between them had already been going on longer than one hot spring night.

'I know this might not seem like it's my business,' Meg said, 'but Dylan is my business, and he's been different this week. He's been spry, and twitchy and far less of a pain in the butt than he has been in years. I have the feeling I have you to thank for it.'

Wynnie's hands shook as she put the butterfly in her purse. 'Perhaps he's so chipper as he's planning on new and wonderful ways of telling me "no". In a professional capacity,' she added as a dismal addendum.

Meg held up a hand, and, being that she was of the same Kelly stock, Wynnie found her words drying up in her mouth.

'Then look at it this way; he's not the be-all and end-all when it comes to making decisions about KInG. My father is the CEO, and our older brother Brendan is all set to take over…' Meg's hand dropped into her lap. 'One day a long, long time from now. So if you're game, I'd love you to come with me as my guest. Give yourself one last chance to make your case.'

Meg Kelly was a clever girl. She'd made the temptation far too great.

Wynnie had one last chance to find out if Dylan was all she so deeply thought he was, or whether her usual bad judgment made her just another notch on the smiling assassin's bedpost.

And one last chance to convince KInG to join with the CFC.

Her cheeks flushed as she realised her first thought had been Dylan, and not how precipitous an opportunity she had just been thrown to get her job done.

Either way, Wynnie couldn't turn Meg down.

'I'd be delighted.' Wynnie smiled at Meg over the top of her drink. 'So why aren't you the vice president of some fabulous company?'

Meg's mouth twisted into a smile. 'If I'd been this age in the eighties—the days of three-hour lunches, junkets overseas and perks up the wazoo—then who knows?'

The door swung open and Rylie flounced in, obviously having heard the tail-end of a story she'd heard before. 'You'd never have carried off the shoulder pads.'

'Oh, well. Too bad. A life of leisure and avoiding making excuses to the fam is to be my lot. Here's my mobile number.' Meg handed over a shiny white business card with a large bold embossed letter *'M'* above a mobile number and an e-mail address in bold hot pink letters. 'Message me your address and I'll swing by and pick you up at yours at say three o'clock and we'll head to the manor from there.'

'Sounds good.'

Meg stood and Wynnie did the same.

'You coming?' Rylie asked Meg, and the two of them bounced out the door, waving their goodbyes.

Wynnie slumped back onto the couch and stared at Meg's card, wondering how on earth she would explain her presence at his family's home to Dylan, and wondering what else she could possibly think to say to him after that.

CHAPTER NINE

DYLAN hid on his hands and knees behind a manicured hedge in the centre of the park at the rear of his parents' Edwardian-style home, ostensibly counting backwards from thirty-eight. That was as high as Olive, Brendan's youngest, knew how to count.

'Ready or not, here I come!' he bellowed after enough time seemed to have passed, and the direction of the squeals that followed told him the girls were both in the exact same places they had been the week before. Didn't mean he couldn't take his time finding them.

It took a loud oomphing sound to make getting up easier.

'Don't do that,' Cameron said as he wandered over, carrying a bone-china plate covered in crumbs that told of intensely delicious hors d'oeuvres, which Dylan was missing out on.

Food had worked a treat the last time he was here and trying to stop thinking about what lay beneath Wynnie's outer layers. Now that he knew the answer in brilliant, intimate detail he feared he might need a table full all for himself.

'You're older than me,' Cameron said. 'You're giving me a bad image of what I might be like in two years.'

Dylan brushed grass off the knees of his casual, hide-and-seek-ready trousers. 'You're married now, remember. I'll give it a year before everyone starts thinking you're older anyway.'

'Nah. My love's glow will keep me ageless and this good-looking forever. You, on the other hand, as a ridiculously determined single man, will wear mismatched socks and lose your car keys and your sentences will be replaced by mumbles. But you'll still be welcome at Rosalind's and mine.' Cam added a slap to the back as he said, 'Old man.'

'Leave me be, I have pre-teens to entertain. Only the cool uncle gets that job. But first tell me where I can get my mouth around some of that food. My stomach needs filling and fast.'

'Not just yet. Meg's here, and she's brought a little friend,' Cameron said with just enough of a smile in his voice Dylan knew the joke was about to be on him.

Dylan glanced up at the house to see his sister and...

His empty stomach went into free fall and landed somewhere in the region of his knees. 'You have got to be kidding me.'

Cameron laughed. 'Don't tell me she's brought an old flame here to haunt you again.'

When Dylan said nothing but continued to stare, Cameron added softly, 'Or perhaps it is a new flame.'

If the fire in his belly had anything to say about it, Cameron was spot on. So much for splitting from the TV studio quick smart to give himself the chance to clear his head of her—to remove himself from her soft warm body, her delectably sharp tongue, her expressive eyes that told him right there on live television that, despite the games, despite the professional gulf between them, she hadn't had enough of him any more than he'd had enough of her. Now the mere sight of her in the distance deluged him with all those intense feelings again like a sudden summer storm.

Nevertheless he rallied to shake his head. 'Less of a flame, more of a thorn in my side.'

Since that morning she'd pinned her fringe from her forehead, leaving her face open and guileless, her waves curling softly against her cheeks. A pale blue and cream lace top gently draped over her shoulders, whispering across her breasts, veering in to show off her small waist and stopping just below the beltline of tight jeans. Her flat silver shoes gave a bounce to her steps.

He'd never seen her look so pretty, so utterly feminine. The latent he-man instincts she always seemed to conjure up flew into overdrive and his skin began to tighten and prickle and hurt.

He curled his fingers into his palms. So far the only way he'd found to make those persistent and highly inconvenient feelings go away was having her naked skin flush against his own. Meaning either he had to make love to her every night for the rest of his life, or this unhealthy relationship had to come to a swift end.

'Dylan,' Cameron mumbled, apparently still beside him.

'What?' he barked.

'Would I be completely wrong in thinking that *you* might be glowing?'

The bark turned to a growl. 'So wrong it makes me wonder if your new wife is not beating you about the head as you sleep. It'd be a fast way for her to come into a quick fortune, you know.'

Cameron's glare was baleful, and Dylan knew he'd over-stepped the mark. He patted his brother on the back and added, 'Though if you snore the way you used to at camp I wouldn't blame her if she did.'

Cameron forgave him with a smile, before moving off in the direction of his new bride. The two of them couldn't seem to be apart for longer than five minutes.

As though Dylan were in need of any other means to add to his now almost constant discomfort, he took a step Wynnie's way but stopped when his mother cut them off. Wynnie's smile seemed genuine as his mother kissed her on the cheek. She said something then that made his mother laugh.

Her hair was fluttering across her face, the breeze sucking her filmy top to her skin shaping every delicious curve until he had no choice but to remember the sheen and tone of every inch of skin.

And those big brown cow eyes just made him melt in

places he didn't know it was possible for a grown man to melt. Thank God the rest of her made the rest of him rock-hard.

He took another step towards the house and stopped again when his father appeared from nowhere to join the welcome party. She shook his hand, looked him in the eye and cocked her head to one side as he told her some story or other. likely about golf, or sailing.

She listened. As though she just knew there was no greater way to Quinn's good graces than to make him think he was fascinating.

As the rest of the gang, bar him, joined in the welcome Wynnie's melodic laughter rang across the lawn. Her bright eyes shone, even from this distance. She showed no fear of the usually amply intimidating group. And as one they bowed towards her like sunflowers to the sun.

Each and every one of them on the board of the Kelly Investment Group.

'Oh, crap,' he said aloud as his blood began to chill in his veins.

No wonder her eyes were yet to seek him out. He was the very last person she had come here to see.

Damn Meg and her meddling. He had to clean up her messes more than everyone else's combined, and right now he wanted to ring her little neck. But she'd have to get in line. Wynnie Devereaux was right up front.

Since the hideous, unscrupulous, malicious break-up with Lilliana, his eyes had been wide-open to the fact that every woman he'd ever known had wanted something from him. Wynnie was no different—she'd just been so upfront about wanting to get into bed with KInG his usually rock-solid guard had slipped. And he'd spent the past week following his groin rather than his gut. Shame on him, twice over.

Brendan, who was leaning against a pillar on the outer rim of the circle, caught his eye over a cup of coffee. He raised an eyebrow before tilting his head in Wynnie's direction.

The Trojan horse might not have made it back inside the building, but she had made it smack bang into the middle of the inner sanctum, and it was entirely his doing.

It all came back to the small pile of photocopied news stories Jack had left him with; Wynnie questioned day after day for twelve days, not because there was any evidence she'd had anything to do with the attack on the laboratory, but because she'd refused to say a word about where her brother might be. Twelve days she'd kept her mouth shut. Not giving up her family to save herself.

He'd held on to that, tightly, as he'd called in a favour to get a ticket to the museum ball. It had thrown him in the way of a swinging fist, and sent him to her bed.

But the truth was he actually had not one clue if she had been involved with radical, violent, environmentalist saboteurs. Video footage and witness evidence said her brother most certainly was. Seven people had been injured that day, including one who was put into a wheelchair for life. And here she was in his home, mixing with his family. He didn't know which direction to step first.

The family split in all directions, and Meg's arm linked through Wynnie's as she took her down onto the grass. Wynnie's eyes skimmed the park until they found his and there they stayed.

Her soft pink lips curved into a private smile, and even from twenty feet away he could see the pink rising in her cheeks.

He gritted his teeth and fought back the urge to throw her over his shoulder and drag her the hell out of there as fast as his legs would carry them.

When he realised he wasn't sure if his desire to do so was about keeping her from getting any closer to his family, or because he wanted to get her alone, he managed to squash his inner Neanderthal, and find enough calming breath to appear cool.

'Dylan,' Meg said, smirking as if she were eight-years-old

and had caught him kissing Katie Finch in the cloisters at the front of the house. 'I believe you know my new friend Wynnie. I picked her up in the green room after Rylie's show. Already I love her to bits.'

'How could you not? She's a jewel.'

He glanced at Wynnie. Her big brown eyes were lit up from the inside. Questions and newfound nerves and attraction skittered behind her gaze but far too quickly to decipher exactly what she was thinking. He blinked at her, his expression a blank mask, hopefully letting her think he didn't care.

'Now we had a great talk in the car on the way here,' Meg babbled, 'all about her work, and I just love what this girl has to say. She's smart, and I know you appreciate smart. So why aren't you being a good boy and doing exactly what you're being told and agree to turn off some lights and fork out on ceramic mugs rather than plastic cups in the office, for Pete's sake?'

Why? Why indeed? Put like that it seemed like the simplest thing in the world for him to do. Hell, he could write a memo in ten seconds flat, and Eric would make it happen before lunch.

But with Wynnie Devereaux standing there before him looking like a wood nymph who'd skipped out of the Kelly Manor's small forest, looking like the woman who'd fallen apart, twice, in his arms less than twenty-four hours earlier, looking like the woman who had skirted the rules again and again to get around him to get to his family, there was no way on God's green earth he was going to say yes.

Wynnie sat on a white cane lounge on the Kellys' immaculate back lawn, shaded by a large cloth sun sail, sipping at a glass of iced tea.

She only listened with half an ear as Quinn Kelly told a story about the time he went on an African safari. Squeals of delight kept her mind focused on the action occurring somewhere over her right shoulder.

The one or two glances she had managed afforded her glimpses of Dylan playing with his two young nieces.

She bit at her left thumbnail, her brow tight from over-furrowing. If she'd had any concerns about the extent and breadth of her feelings for Dylan after the way he'd made love to her the night before, the image of him running in random circles chasing down two adorable girls in pigtails, not caring if he got grass stains on his trousers or their gorgeous pastel dresses, magnified every trepidation tenfold.

The back of her hair suddenly began to itch, and she was sure she was being watched. Not only watched, *stared* at.

The burning feeling moved down her neck, between her shoulder blades, over her hips, caressing her thighs. She sucked in a deep shaky breath and willed herself not to turn around, not to check to see if it was all in her head.

Her will was obviously not nearly as strong as her curiosity. She flicked her hair off her face and shot a quick glance over her shoulder to find Dylan throwing a soft ball from one hand to another, watching her as the girls ran off in opposite directions.

She searched his eyes for the heat she'd felt, but they were closed to her. She gave him a discreet nod. It took longer than was in any way comfortable for him to do the same back.

Maybe if she'd been able to corner him for a minute before his family had cornered her she could have told him this was all Meg's idea. That she'd never had any intention of storming the family compound on her quest to rid the world of incandescent light globes. Perhaps he might not look at her quite so darkly.

Her heart reached out to him. Imploring her to let it do its thing. To care, to want more for herself, to love… To give him the chance to do the same, no matter how great the probability her job, his stubbornness, her fear of getting close, whatever lingering issues he still had with his ex-fiancée all meant that she would get hurt as usual.

She'd never felt the way she felt with Dylan when she'd been with any other man. Or with any other person, for that matter. With him she felt as though parts of herself that had never seen the light of day were now in full bloom.

His dark eyes slid past hers as though she were of no more interest to him than the chair she sat upon.

Her heart sank. Then again, maybe a minute's conversation wouldn't make a lick of difference.

'Don't you think?'

Quinn's deep drawl echoed on the periphery of Wynnie's mind. She turned back to find him watching her with a question in his pale blue eyes.

The only answer she could think in that moment was, 'Right. Of course.'

Brendan leant forwards to grab a napkin, his eyes barely touching hers before he said, 'Dad I'm not sure if you realise this was the one who handcuffed herself to our sculpture a few days back.'

Wynnie felt her neck warm. Dealing with Dylan might have been like bouncing between a rock and a hard place, but she certainly had no ally in Brendan.

Meg grinned at Wynnie, her eyes twinkling as she silently encouraged her to leap in, but as far as she could tell Meg held little sway. She was treated like the princess, not allowed to lift a finger even when she wanted to.

The silver fox, Quinn Kelly, might be her only hope.

'Ah-h-h,' Quinn said, looking at her as though for the first time. 'The Trojan horse.'

She glanced back at Meg hoping to make sense of the comment, but Meg just shrugged.

'Okay, Ms Devereaux, you've made it further than anyone else in your position has ever made it before. I'll give you props for ingenuity. So tell me, why should we spend our time and money reorganising the meticulously efficient way we believe we do business when the largest, richest industrial states in the world aren't bothering?'

Her last chance. With Dylan, and with the Kellys. Dylan

was sending burning arrows into the back of her head; Quinn Kelly was giving her five minutes. The way she saw it she didn't have a choice.

Wynnie sat up straighter in her high chair, clasped her hands atop her knees and looked every one of them in the eye as she said, 'I love ice cream.'

'Ice cream,' Brendan repeated, deadpan, but at least she knew he was listening.

'I lo-o-ove ice cream,' Meg said. 'I'd eat it for breakfast, lunch and dinner if I had my way.'

'Vanilla ice cream is my all-time favourite,' Cameron said, before sending goo-goo eyes at his wife.

She opened her mouth to move on when the scent of clean linen and fresh-cut grass washed over her in a wave of heat.

A large hand curled over the back of her chair, fingers stopping against her shoulder blade, the effect of the touch sluicing much further.

'What did I miss?' Dylan asked from behind her.

'We were having a lovely discussion about ice cream,' his mother said, all politeness.

Wynnie leant forwards ever so slightly but enough that she could focus on her pitch. Four minutes. She could see in Quinn Kelly's eyes that was all she had. And even with Dylan glowering and breathing down her neck, she was in so deep already she was going to use every one of them.

'I love ice cream,' Wynnie repeated. 'In fact, my love affair with the stuff could be considered counter-productive.'

Dylan snorted. Her cheeks warmed, she gritted her teeth, and crossed her legs away from his general direction.

She smiled at Mary, who was smiling at her. 'So I always buy low fat. My friend Hannah rolls her eyes and tells me if I truly wanted to make a difference to my waistline I wouldn't eat the stuff at all. But I know myself too well for all that. I will eat ice cream. So I figure if I can do a little bit of good by choosing low fat, then that's a step in the right direction.'

'Here! Here!' Meg shouted, winking at her.

Wynnie gave her a quick smile before directing her next words to Brendan, to Cameron, to Quinn. 'The same logic applies to all sorts of occurrences in our daily lives. We all use clothes dryers when it's wet outside, we heat our towels on the column heater before getting out of the shower on a cold winter's morning, we buy plastic packaging, we get our bills in the mail. But if we all also remembered to unplug any appliances that aren't being used, if we recycled our newspapers and milk bottles, received bills and memos via e-mail not envelope, that's a step in the right direction. Just by doing a little bit of good.'

The table was quiet. Too quiet. Her heart began to thud as she tried to decipher from the brilliant poker faces around her if she'd made it through.

With thirty seconds up her sleeve she uncrossed her legs, sat forward knocking her knees and letting her hands talk for her. 'I grew up in a place where the people were drawn to the principles of permaculture, of living off whatever the community could produce. My family saw this as a way of taking responsibility for their existence, so this stuff is not new to me. But I'm just like you. I eat meat. I wear leather. I like fishing. I'm not suggesting we all live in eco-bubbles and eat nothing but spinach. I just think we can *all* try a little harder to think not only of ourselves but the wider community, as well.'

Quinn's eyebrows slowly rose. 'To not only think of ourselves, did she say?' He shot a look at his wife. 'Do you think that was a direct jibe at our lot?'

Mary's smile was wide and genuine. 'If so, it was a fair one.'

Wynnie released a long slow breath and planted her shaking feet firmly on the ground. She'd been accused once upon a time of pushing too hard, of getting too close, she could only hope she hadn't done it again. Or if she had, this time it had worked.

When Quinn clicked his fingers and a man appeared as if from a hole in the ground, he asked for more iced tea, and Wynnie knew she wasn't about to be kicked out on her rear.

Quinn turned back to her, his eyes smiling. 'So, Wynnie, tell me, where did you grow up?'

The question was so unexpected she sat there in stunned silence. She had brought it up, in a round-about kind of way, but the details were something she'd much prefer not going into lest her past and her present begin to intersect—

'Nimbin.' Dylan's deep voice rang loud and clear in her right ear as he leant over and grabbed a condensation-covered glass of his own. He took a long slow sip before adding, 'She grew up in Nimbin.'

'Get out of here!' Meg hollered, cutting into her thoughts. 'The land of milk and hemp. I always thought that place was some kind of myth.'

'So Nimbin's where they grow consciences nowadays,' Quinn said with the kind of smile that would have made Wynnie blush if her cheeks weren't already so filled with a rush of blood they felt as if they were burning.

'Her parents were newlyweds,' Dylan continued, leaning lazily against the arm of her chair—filling her personal space with his warmth, his size, his shadow. 'They attended the Aquarius Festival on their honeymoon and stayed, living off what they grew themselves and home-schooling their kids.'

'Oh,' Mary said, 'so you have brothers and sisters?'

Wynnie's feet suddenly felt as though they were no longer touching the ground. She had to grip the arms of her chair lest she slide right out of it onto the grass.

But Dylan didn't, he couldn't *possibly* know—

'One brother,' he answered for her, and her throat burned as though it suddenly filled with bile.

She glanced up at him to find his face was haloed by the bright light of the setting sun. But he was no angel. He was the devil incarnate. Somehow he knew her darkest secrets. How long he'd known them she had no idea.

But she did know that in that moment he was showing his

cards. If he saw the need to do so, he would use her secrets in any way he saw fit.

As if realising she was close enough to physically hurt him if she saw fit, Dylan drifted away.

'I'm glad to hear it,' Mary Kelly's voice murmured in a fuzzy corner of Wynnie's shut-down brain. 'Family is everything. If more people realised that, then feeling a part of a wider community would naturally ensue.'

Quinn stood, his wife was at his side in a lightning flash, cradling his elbow. Wynnie lifted slightly off her chair wondering if he needed help.

But Mary's beatific smile made her realise it was love that had her at her husband's side, not anything more sinister.

'I like you,' Quinn said, patting her on the shoulder. 'I hope Dylan sees the light and lets you in. KInG has become far too stuffy these past months.' And then he and his wife were heading slowly back to the house.

Dylan? she repeated in her head. *He hoped Dylan would see the light? But—*

Brendan cleared his throat and shot her a quick smile as he stood, as well. 'Nice pitch, Ms Devereaux. Inventive as all get out. If you're ever looking to get a real job, give me a call.'

Meg glanced over her shoulder before flouncing away from the table. 'Don't go anywhere,' she said. 'I'll be back. I just have to make a phone call. Great job, though. A whole afternoon and I haven't been the centre of attention once!'

Cameron and his wife, Rosie, had quietly disappeared some time around the first mention of ice cream, meaning Wynnie had been left alone to try to pick up the pieces of what had just happened.

She pulled herself from her chair and spun to find Dylan a metre away. His eyes were blank, his stance far too cool for a man who had just quietly proven he could ruin her life with a word if it suited him.

Her fingers curled into her palms so that she didn't do as

she so wanted to do and slap some life back into his beautiful aloof face.

'They never had any intention of giving me a chance, did they?' she asked, her voice husky, skirting the subject that truly ate her up.

'Of course not. They'd never side with someone outside the family over me.'

A glint lit his eyes. She reacted to it physically as she always had. She slapped down the rising heat and thought cold thoughts, such as how it might feel if she encased his large bare feet in concrete and dropped him to the floor of the Arctic Ocean.

She waved a hand towards the big house which was mostly hidden by the sun sail above her head. 'Yet you just stood there and let me make my pitch to them, knowing it wouldn't make a lick of difference.'

'Would you have kept mum if I'd asked you to?'

She knew the answer was no, so she bit her tongue and just glared at him instead.

'And how the hell did you know all that other stuff about… me?' She paced back and forth and waved her arms about her head so fast she felt like a helicopter preparing to take off.

He sipped at his drink. 'I had you investigated.'

Her blood turned to acid in her veins. 'You what?'

Then she realised if it wasn't because she'd slipped and told him more than she should have in her weaker moments around him, then he probably knew everything.

He slid his spare hand into his pocket and downed the last of his drink, his tanned throat working with every swallow. The fact that she could still find him sexy, even now, scared the hell out of her.

'There's no point in being all sanctimonious about this, Wynnie. I'd bet my house on the fact that you had me researched to the nth degree before deciding I was the one you had to have.'

Her pacing range shortened but didn't lessen in fury one bit. 'So when you leapt in all heroic and saved me from the big bad reporter who knew my real name—'

'You mean, last night.'

She flapped a hand at him, as if it didn't matter that it had been less than twenty-four hours since he'd spent hours kissing every inch of her that he possibly could. As if that weren't the crux from which all this new tension between them had sprung.

'You knew everything,' she continued. 'You weren't protecting me from him. You were saving the information for when you might need it yourself.'

This time he didn't argue, didn't interject. Because she'd hit the mark dead centre.

The moist grass squished beneath her shoes and she replayed every conversation they'd ever had, every time she'd thought she'd had the upper hand, every moment he'd treated her body as if it were the most beautiful thing he had ever seen.

Her pacing stopped; she faced him, crossed her arms and asked, 'Tell me the truth. Right here and now. Have you been playing me all along?'

He blinked. The shutters cleared. The man behind the dangerously charming mask appeared.

Her heart reached out to him, begging him to stay, to break through. But all too soon the glint in his eyes returned and he was lost behind the practised blue haze.

She said, 'From the moment you walked out into that forecourt and gave me that seductive little smile, from when you sent Eric to check your iron to get me alone, and our dance, when you let what's-his-name punch you first, and let me play nursemaid, and let me...' She had to stop to take a breath. Letting him see how important last night had been was not in her best interests in that moment. 'Has every second been a game to you?'

His cheek curved, her stomach dropped and he said, 'Have I ever done anything to make you think it hasn't?' He took a second to let his eyes rest on her left shoulder, the curve of her waist, her right thigh. His hot dark eyes were locked right on hers as he finished the thought.

She blinked up at him, the memories flooding over her, replacing bad thoughts with good. No man who made love like that could possibly be all bad.

'Dylan,' she said, her voice imploring.

But the shutters came back down over his cold blue eyes—bang, bang.

She threw her hands in the air, spun on her heel and stalked away towards the side of the big house.

Coming here had been a mistake. To badger him into listening to what she had to say about her life's work was one thing, to allow him to see her in a moment when her heart felt as if it were beating outside her chest was just plain reckless.

She heard his footfalls right behind her. 'Stop following me.'

'I'm not, we're just going in the same direction and you're so small my strides eat yours for breakfast.'

'Ha! Like you'd have a clue what I eat for breakfast. You were out of there so fast last night you left skid marks in your wake. Oh, sorry. I'd forgotten, your investigator probably gave you a rundown on how I like that, as well!'

His fingers wrapped around her elbow, slowing her down. She twisted her arm away. He slid an arm about her waist instead, turning her to face him, and the guy had such a hold her only way out would be to slip to her knees and crawl.

She pushed her hands against his chest, dug her toes into her shoes and glared at him. Let him speak next. Let him find another new way to prove to her that she was damned to choose very, very badly when she chose to love.

She squeezed her eyes shut tight lest he see the startling realisation that had been slowly dawning on her all the long day.

He said, 'We both knew what we were getting into last night.'

Her laughter was slightly hysterical.

'Look at me,' he demanded.

Her eyes flew open; she glared at him for all she was worth.

'We are combatants on a field of play,' he said. 'And last night we simply took a moment's armistice. If that's all it was, then there is nothing wrong with that.'

He reached out and tucked his hand into her hair, and again she felt his eyes looking for answers in hers while only he knew the question.

His suddenly hot gaze trailed down her face to rest on her lips. 'Nothing at all.'

Before she even had the chance to draw breath, he drew her in, and he kissed her. Hard, soundly, in a way meant to wipe anything from her mind but him.

She fought against the instant rising waves of heat lapping against her stomach, her breasts, her throat. But when her hands began to soften against his solid chest she was gone.

Her fingers curled into his T-shirt and pulled him closer as she pressed herself along his pitilessly rock-hard length.

They kissed as though every word, every smile, every clash between them thus far had been foreplay. Wild, unchecked, hopeless passion sent Wynnie's senses spiralling away from her and over the edge of reason.

When there was nothing reminding her who and where she was but a speck of sunlight far, far away in the corner of her mind, she somehow managed to drag herself back to the surface. Not nearly soon enough.

She glared at his rising and falling chest as sense returned like a slap to the back of the head. 'I knew you were hard,' she said, her voice red raw, 'but I never thought you could be cruel. No matter how much you might want me gone, you should never have used sex as a weapon.'

His smouldering eyes cooled until they were lit as though by chips of ice. 'Honey—'

'Don't call me "Honey",' she shot back, 'like I'm some kind of interchangeable body to warm your bed. Like I'm not important enough for you to bother knowing my name.'

'Fine,' he said, 'Guinevere.'

She reared back as though slapped, and he let her go. She stumbled now he no longer held her up.

A butterfly fluttered past her nose. Beautiful, fragile, its days numbered. With it she found her centre.

'If I'm right,' she said, 'and you have all sorts of juicy information in that dossier of yours, you'll know that I am an abnormally forgiving person, even of those who have used me and hurt me more than one person deserves to be hurt. But right this second, I am looking forward to the day you rot in hell.'

Energy surged through her, giving her the impetus to finally walk away.

Wynnie all but ran as she rounded the side of the house. She'd send Mary a note thanking her for lunch, but right now she couldn't face a one of them.

As always happened when she walked away from him she felt Dylan's eyes burning a trail down the length of her body.

Only this time it didn't fill her with the kind of sexual energy that would keep her going all day. This time it felt like goodbye.

CHAPTER TEN

ON THURSDAY evening Wynnie trudged up her lushly over-grown footpath, her eyes feeling full of grit after not having slept properly in days, her feet sore from wearing high heels for twelve hours at a time as she worked herself senseless, her throat dry from the hundred odd cold calls she'd made in the past four days trying to line up preliminary interviews with the heads of every big company in town.

That was all she deserved for screwing up so badly with the only company she'd even thought about reeling in. Falling into bed with the target; what had she been thinking?

She slammed open the mouth of her neat white mailbox and grabbed the mail as vehemently as such a thing could be done.

Once inside the cottage, she kicked off her slinky red high heels, checked her phone messages to find the one from Meg from a few days back had *still* not been deleted from the ruddy machine.

'*I saw you kissing after lunch,*' Meg's lilting voice called through the small speaker. '*Don't worry. It was only me peeking out the window. The rest of them are far too self-involved to have noticed a thing. I just wanted to say "yay"! And even though D's a right pain, he needs someone like you to keep him in line. See ya soon!*'

She jabbed a finger at the machine, several times, until it read zero messages. But, knowing she'd only have to hear the damn message again the next day, she pulled the cord out of the wall.

Punishment. That was what her life had become. An endless round of paying for her mistakes.

It had been four days since she'd laid eyes on Dylan Kelly. Four days since she'd heard his voice, been witness to his sexy smile, and her heart still felt as bruised as if she'd walked away from him five minutes ago.

Absently rubbing her right foot up her aching left calf, she threw her mail on the dining table and flicked through it. Junk mail, pay-TV-overdue-account reminder addressed to the previous tenants, and the thick familiar feel of a postcard.

Her foot slid to the floor. She needed them both flat on the ground for this. Her blood thundered in her ears and her breath released on the one word: 'Felix.'

She ran her thumb over the shiny picture on the front. Palm trees. Blue water. White sand. Tahiti.

She didn't need to turn the postcard over to know it was from him, but she did anyway. As always hoping for a message, some kind of word on where he was, what he was doing, that he was safe.

And as always the back side was blank, bar a stamp, her address written in someone else's hand, and a postmark from of all places, Lima. It would only lead to a dead end.

She slumped till her backside rested against the dining table.

More punishment to add to the rest. A teasing reminder that she had someone out there who was meant to be on her side no matter what, but she couldn't have any contact with him. And a thump to the heart reminding her that she had let herself be denigrated, torn apart, broken down all to save his guilty hide.

And all she ever got for her troubles was a batch of blank postcards.

She flicked her hair off her face and her eyes fell on the chocolate-brown couch with the red angora rug draped lazily over it.

Postcards and a string of bad decisions when it came to knowing who to trust. And for the first time in her life the ache to see her brother again had less to do with love for him than it had to do with wanting to shake the breath out of the little punk and make sure he had a clue how he'd messed up her life.

She threw the postcard onto the pile of junk mail, and headed into the kitchen. There she found a bottle of red wine and a large glass and took them both into her bedroom.

Wynnie cradled a glass of red wine, her third, in her palm as she sat cross-legged in the middle of her bed, still dressed in the off-the-shoulder, belted, short black dress she'd worn to work.

Her phone lay at the tip of her bare right foot, Felix's post-card at the top of the left, and a phone number scribbled on the back of an old receipt clutched in her spare hand.

She'd been staring at the phone number for a good hour already. She'd even managed to get halfway through it before hanging up twice.

She put her wine on the bedside table; it only sloshed a very little before steadying. She shook out her hands, cricked her neck, picked up her phone and dialled.

It rang once. She took such a deep breath she started to see stars on the edge of her vision.

It rang twice. She closed her eyes and bounced up and down on the spot to try to release the influx of energy surging through her body.

An all too familiar male voice answered. 'Hello?'

She stopped bouncing, her eyes flew open. Her voice cracked, just a little, as she said, 'Dylan?'

A long pause. Then, 'Wynnie.'

The sound of his voice was like an elixir, warming all the cold places inside her. She drew her knees to her chest and wrapped her arms about her shins, trying to keep the remarkable feeling locked inside as long as she could.

She closed her eyes and a stray tear slid down her cheek. She hastily swiped it away, knowing it would probably taste of Cab Sav. 'Look, I'm truly sorry to ring you like this. Mortified, in fact. But I called Meg and asked for your number and she gave it to me.'

She thought she'd sounded perfectly fine but he must have picked up an off note as his voice came back to her strong, determined, and most of all, protective. 'Wynnie, what's wrong? Are you all right? What's happened?'

'Nothing's wrong.' Nothing new anyway. 'I just had a question that couldn't keep. It's not a work question so I didn't want to bother you during work hours.'

'Since when did propriety become your catchphrase?' he asked, his voice now liquid sex, as if he hadn't been a coldhearted bastard and she hadn't told him to rot in hell when they'd last seen one another.

It hurt, it ached, it made her hold herself tighter, but at least he hadn't hung up.

Not sure she would be able to cope with any more complications to her life in that minute she decided to get to the point. 'It's about you having had me investigated.'

'We've been over this,' he said.

She waved her hand in front of her face as though he could see her. He stopped talking as though he could, too.

'I know,' she said. 'I just… There's something…'

'Just ask.'

She closed her eyes and this time tears poured down her face. 'My brother. Do you know where he is?'

'Wynnie—'

'I don't care how you know,' she said on a rush of garbled air. 'I don't care if you have my bank account passwords, statements from my kindergarten teachers, or my bra size on file. I really don't give a flying hoot at this point in time. I just need to know about Felix. I have to see him. I need to talk to him, to know if he's all right.' *To let him know I'm not.* 'So if you know anything, anything at all, I need you to tell me.'

Her breaths came laboured and deep and she gripped so tight to the phone her fingers ached, and years worth of sorry tears continued pouring down her cheeks.

His voice was gruff when he asked, 'Where are you?'

'Home.' She sniffed.

'Don't go anywhere.'

'Dylan—'

'I'm coming over.'

He hung up.

She stared at the phone through her steamy eyes. She gave a great big sniff, wiped frantically at her face and tried calling back, but there was no answer.

She threw the phone on the bed and rubbed her face hard.

Why had she ever thought she might get what she wanted from him, ever? He was so damned contrary!

The moment she'd reconciled herself to not having him she got him. And when she knew how much she wanted him, she couldn't have him.

She lay back on the bed with a thump and stared at the wide, still ceiling fan.

But when she *needed* him…he came.

Fifteen minutes later Wynnie was pacing the living-room floor, her bare feet making sharp slapping sounds on the wood, when a loud rap sounded at her door.

Her disobedient heart rapped even louder against her ribs. Four days. Four days without seeing him, and despite everything her heart raced like an excited puppy.

She took a deep breath. She'd open the door, she'd show him she was fine, tell him she'd had a glass too many and should never have called, and then he'd think badly of her—nothing new there—and leave.

She opened the door, expecting to find herself faced with

the pitiless suit. But there he stood in a crushed white long-sleeved T-shirt poking out of the bottom of an old-fashioned black blazer and old jeans that fell soft at the knees, frayed and splayed at the hem, and clung lovingly everywhere else.

In a suit he was devastating. Dressed down, as though he was trying to blend in with regular folk, only showcased how truly beautiful he was.

'Dylan,' she croaked, 'go home.'

His blue eyes were dark. His cheeks tight. His mouth a thin horizontal line. 'Not until I know that you're okay.'

She shrugged. 'That's not your concern.'

His cheek twitched. But he didn't contradict her. Her heart gave a sorry little tug.

'Either way, I'm here now, so why don't you just let me in?'

And then from behind his back he pulled a bucket of ice cream. Dairy Bell's Nuts About Chocolate, the most decadent ice cream in the history of ice cream. 'You never mentioned your favourite flavour but this was always Meg's favourite when she was having a "crapola day". Her words.'

She took the ice cream and cradled it under her arm, the cold good for her. It helped keep the heat he aroused in her veins from going to her head.

'I shouldn't have called.'

'Yet you did.'

Her next breath in was unsteady. The fact that this man knew *everything* about her was a relationship she'd never experienced before. Hannah knew pieces. But Hannah didn't know her grief and her guilt. This man did.

Yet he wasn't her friend. He wasn't even her lover. He was a compulsion, an illusion, a threat.

But she was so tired. Tired of keeping secrets, and watching her words, and holding on so tight to her life lest all the disparate pieces got carried away by the lightest gust of wind.

He knew everything. Telling him more couldn't hurt. Maybe, with his connections, it might even help.

'I could do with a coffee,' he said, his eyes boring into hers. 'And your ice cream's melting.'

She stood back and let him in.

They sat at the dining table. Dylan at the head, silently watching Wynnie on her chair pulled at an angle from the side of the table. Her knees were hugged to her chest, the spoon with which she'd eaten half the tub of ice cream resting against her mouth, her eyes roaming over a spread-out stack of mail on the table.

Her black dress draped from one shoulder leaving it exposed. Her hair was pinned off her face, her long fringe sweeping across her brow. Her eyes were dark and smudged. Her skin as pale as milk. Her lips bare.

She'd never looked more beautiful, or more fragile. And that was the combination that got him into trouble with her again and again.

Dylan held tight to his cold coffee mug to make sure his hands didn't rove anywhere else, and questioned himself for about the tenth time what he was doing there. Even though looking back he was conscious he had overreacted and overcomplicated what had only been a night of great sex, the result, their parting, had been for the best.

'When Felix was little,' she said as though they were mid-conversation about the guy, not that it was the first time his name had been mentioned since Dylan had arrived, 'he couldn't pronounce Guinevere. He called me Wynnie. So when the police finally told me they were done with me, when I knew I had to have a fresh start, somewhere to wash off that whole experience, I began by shedding the name that had been splashed all over the papers, took my grandmother's surname and chose a new path.'

She stuck a finger in her mouth and nibbled on the end. Her lips shone with moisture. Her eyes blinked languidly as her memories took her far away. Dylan pressed his feet hard into the floor, and kept his focus from the couch lurking just over her bare right shoulder. From their one night of phenomenal sex.

'I like the name Guinevere,' she said, her eyes suddenly focusing and swinging to his, full of accusation.

He held up both hands in surrender. 'It's a beautiful name. French?'

She blinked again, and then her cheek lifted into a slow half-smile. 'I think the name is old French but I have no idea beyond that. What's with you and the French thing?'

'It's the accent. It speaks to my G-spot.'

'Mmm. Well, all I know is that Guinevere means fair and smooth. Does that work for you?'

'Don't ask. And Felix?' Time to bring the conversation where it needed to be. Flirting, though so very difficult not to engage in around this woman, was not helpful.

'Happy,' she said on a ragged sigh.

He furrowed his brow.

'His name means happy. And he was as a kid. Joyful, and interested and just the sweetest thing on the planet. But after my parents passed away I moved to the city to go to uni and he stayed behind to finish school with his friends around him and… I don't know. He must have fallen in with some radical types who saw Nimbin as a breeding ground for their bionomical army.'

She frowned at the pile of mail again.

'Then what happened?' he asked.

He knew the nuts and bolts. He'd read the papers Jack had given him, more than once in an effort to figure her out. But she *needed* to tell him. *That* was why she'd called. And despite his warnings to her on the contrary, it seemed they both somehow recognised she'd be safer telling him than anyone else.

Her finger slid from her mouth to slowly swipe her fringe back from her eyes, but one stray lock fell straight back down. 'He broke into a science lab attached to the uni, in an effort to let the lab rabbits free. Rabbits, of all things. Environmental pests in Queensland. Anyway, the lab was ransacked, chemicals mixed, an explosion occurred, injuring seven. One man…' She paused, swallowed. 'One man lost the use of his legs. Eco-terrorism, they called it, and they had it all on security tape. They showed me his sweet face. And when they couldn't find him, they came after me.'

'Where did he go?'

She shook her head, shrugged, her eyes turning the exact liquid brown that made his heart feel as if it were sinking and flying all at the same time.

'Our parents had money before they moved to Nimbin and left us the lot when they died. Enough Felix could travel, and hide, his whole life if he so desired.'

'Have you heard from him since?'

Her eye twitched. He felt her drawing inside herself, away from him. He knew that feeling. Closing ranks against all but family. It was an instinct that was hard to break.

She said, 'If I hear from him I am supposed to call the police immediately.'

It was an answer that Dylan philosophically understood. But it didn't stop his stomach from contracting in disappointment as she gently pushed him away.

He ran a hard hand across his mouth. It wasn't as though he deserved her trust. He'd threatened to abuse it so many times.

Then she held up a postcard. A tacky beach setting that ought to have had nude sunbathers on it. 'Every few months I get one,' she said. 'Meaning he knows exactly where I am and what I'm doing. But they never give me one damn clue as to where he is.'

'This is from him?' He took the card, turned it over, frowned at the lack of message. This was the thanks she got from the brother whose life she probably saved by giving him the chance to get the hell out of Dodge?

She nodded. 'It came today.'

So much for pushing him away. Her life had hit a hurdle too high to climb alone and she'd called on him.

This woman had the kind of guts he couldn't even imagine. What she'd done for her brother and how she'd created a life from the ashes of her family splitting apart showed courage. But now, the blind faith she showed in him that she trusted he was man enough not to screw her over, knocked the wind from his sails big-time.

He silently gave the card back. She flicked at a corner, again and again, then held it in her lap.

She watched him down the last of his second cup of coffee. She sniffed in deep and let her feet fall to the floor. She sat on her hands and leant forward, her dress draping and shifting across her pale skin.

Finally she looked down at her bare toes, hot-red toenails blinking back up at her. 'I've never told anybody what I told you just now.'

'I can understand why.'

'And you do realise you could run me out of town with what you know.'

He nodded, his mouth turned down. 'I could. But then I would never again wake up in the morning, wondering if you might be about to leap out of my laundry basket. My life would become ever so dull.'

She lifted her head, squinted at him through one eye, and even managed half a smile.

He didn't take his eyes away. He couldn't.

He'd tried to put her from his mind after Sunday's fiasco. He'd tried immersing himself deep into the job that had kept him more than satisfied his whole adult life. He'd tried to appear attentive when Eric gave him the briefs on each new Wynnie wannabe who called, or wrote requesting a formal meeting with him.

But everything seemed to remind him of her strapped to his sculpture with her crazy cheap handcuffs. Of her turning up at his at his coffee shop with bandages wrapped about her tiny wrists. Of how deeply she believed in what she did. Or how thoroughly she had given herself up to him the moment she'd decided that was what she wanted.

She'd called and he'd come. There hadn't been any hesitation. And now that he was here he suddenly wanted to be the man she obviously thought he was. He needed to be.

He leant forwards and held out a hand. She placed her small hand in his. He looked her square in the eye as he said, 'I'm really sorry but I don't know where he is.'

Her throat worked, her eyes shone, her hand in his turned cold. So cold, he wrapped both of his around hers. He saw the torment in her eyes, and wanted to make it his own. But he just couldn't. His plate was overfull looking after those in his life who were his to take care of whether he wanted to or not.

No wonder he'd railed against her when she'd so neatly backed him into a corner the day they first met. It wasn't altogether fun being shown with such clarity how he'd spent his entire life doing the very same thing to himself.

'Okay,' she said on the end of a deep breath in. 'Then that's that.'

She pulled her hand away and leant back in the chair.

He curled his empty fingers into his palm. He hadn't done enough. And he never could.

He was smart enough to have figured out over the past couple of hours what *enough* might entail. That which he now sensed she wanted from him was simply not his to give. He could be tough if she needed tough, he could be self-deprecating if she needed a smile, he could be kind if she needed a break.

But not even for those demanding liquid brown eyes could he again be naïve enough to promise himself to one woman and mean it.

Yet if he walked out of there and didn't at least give her back half the trust she'd given him, he'd never be able to look himself in the mirror again.

He leant his elbows on the table and looked into his coffee mug as though hoping to find the words therein.

'I'm not claiming to have a clue what you went through back then. But I have had had my dirty laundry aired in public once before.'

She leant her elbows on the table, as well, her chin rested on her upturned palms, and she waited for him to go on.

He said, 'I was engaged once, before.'

He flicked her a glance. She gave him a short smile.

'Lilliana Girard was her name.'

'French?' she asked.

He coughed out an unexpected laugh. 'She would have given her right thumb to stake that claim, but no.'

'Sorry. I couldn't help myself. Go on.'

'We were together for three years. Engaged for one of those. And six weeks before the wedding it hit the papers that she'd quizzed a nightclub full of patrons about which European beach resort she ought to move to when she scored millions in the divorce.'

Wynnie cringed and sucked in a slow stream of air between her lips. Soft pouting lips the colour of dusky pink summer roses. Lips that Lilliana would have killed for. Or had they married she would have used his good money to pay for.

'That's harsh,' Wynnie said. 'Are you sure it wasn't a stupid joke? We girls can do silly things after too many drinks. Add a working phone and I'm living proof.'

He shook his head. 'If only it was the alcohol speaking. Once the story broke, people came out of everywhere quoting conversations had, conversations heard, money owed all over town on the proviso she would take care of it all once she was a Kelly.'

Her eyes grew large with shock. 'She *was* a succubus.'

He laughed again. 'That she was. Now I just feel sorry for her. Three years of her life she spent with a man she didn't really love all for the sake of the *stuff* that came with the name of Kelly.'

She dropped one hand to the table. 'And you didn't have the luxury of changing your name and moving away.'

He looked into her eyes. Deep as an ocean. Warm as a blanket. Clear as a summer sky. 'No, I did not.'

Her other hand slid into her chocolate-brown hair, and his fingers began to tingle. 'It can't be easy assuming every new person in your life just wants something from you.'

She'd hit the nail so directly on the head his whole body clanged like metal on metal. Habit had him leaning lazily back in his chair so she wouldn't notice. 'You know what, it's easier than you think.'

Her arms stretched out straight in front of her. This time it was his turn to lay a hand in hers.

'Thank you,' she said, her brow furrowed, her expression earnest.

'What for?'

'For coming over. For not trying to prolong my hope about Felix, thinking that might help. For telling me about Lilliana.'

'You're welcome.'

'You're a good guy.'

'Now don't go thinking nice things about me. You'll only be disappointed.'

She shook her head. 'You have a good heart. You should use it more often.'

'For the betterment of mankind?'

'Why not?'

Her fingers curled around his, weaving in and out, warming them, leaving them bare, creating enough friction in his hands alone to set the rest of him ablaze.

Her constant ability to believe he had a noble side to him was one of the rare pleasant surprises of believing the worst. And one of the reasons he had to slide his hands away and stand.

'Now it's getting late.'

'So it is.' She tilted her head and smiled up at him and it took every ounce of self-control he had not to kneel down before her and kiss his way up those cruelly tempting bare legs, starting with the hot-red toenails.

'And it is a school night,' he added.

'Right you are.' She pushed herself upright with all the energy of someone who'd just run a marathon.

She padded to the front door. He followed. Her petite form filled out her tiny dress to perfection. Her hips swayed adorably with each footfall. Against the black of her dress her pale skin glowed. The nakedness from her neck to that one bare shoulder cried out to be stroked.

She turned at the door, her hands behind her back clasping the handle. But the door remained closed.

He clenched his back teeth and shoved his hands into the pockets of his jeans. 'Are you going to be okay?'

She nodded, shrugged, then shook her head. 'Eventually.'

She blinked fast as her eyes focused in the middle of his chest. When she looked back at him he knew what she was going to say before she even said it.

'Wynnie——' he warned, trying to cut her off.

But she pushed away from the door and padded to him, stopping only when she was close enough he could make out every eyelash, every fleck of colour in her beautiful eyes, every nuance of desire she felt for him.

Her voice cracked when she said, 'I don't want to be alone tonight.'

All the blood in his body shot to the region of his fly. Well, almost all—enough oxygen flittered around his brain for him to give himself one last shot at actually being noble. 'I left out the fact that I now know there was good reason for Lilliana to have never loved me, you know.'

She blinked up at him, unmoved.

'I'm a cold-hearted bastard. I'm insular, I'm jaded, a workaholic, I'm ruthless and I'm self-serving. I don't do forever, I rarely even do "I'll call you tomorrow". And just because I'm here now it does not mean if you ask me to stay I will.'

She reached up and placed a soft hand on his chest. He breathed in deep, which only filled his nostrils with her sweet scent. This woman, this persistent, tangled, beautiful woman who saw him not just as a Kelly, but as the man who could help her save the world.

She repeated, 'I don't want to be alone tonight.'

The breath bled from his lungs, and his self-control along with it. 'Then you don't have to be.'

CHAPTER ELEVEN

WITHOUT another word, Wynnie took Dylan by the hand and led him into her bedroom.

White furniture, white linen, white lilies in a vase on the dresser. The only splash of colour came from a fat potted palm in the corner.

She reached up and stroked a finger down his cheek and his eyes slid back to her. 'But I need you to know I didn't go to your parents' place on Sunday to pitch the proposal to them.'

He brushed her hair behind her ear. 'I know.'

Her right cheek lifted into the sexiest smile he'd ever seen. He ran his thumb over the dimple it left behind. 'And I didn't have you investigated so that I could use your background against you.'

'You didn't?'

His smile was rueful. At least she was smart enough to doubt him—that made him feel slightly less of a cad. He slid the butterfly clip from the chignon at the back of her head and let her hair fall through his fingers. 'You intrigued me to the point of distraction. I needed something to make you go away.'

She swallowed. 'I'm guessing you found one or two.'

His hand cupped her chin as his eyes slid to hers. 'You're guessing wrong.'

'For a pair of professional communicators, we both have a lot to learn.'

'Mmm. Let this be lesson number one.' He leant down to her, slowly, carefully. His tongue darted out to wet his lips, and just as her eyes fluttered closed he kissed her. Feather-light.

The subtlety of the touch was the most exquisite kind of hell, and no less than he deserved for giving into his irrepressible desire for her right when she was at her most vulnerable.

He kissed her again, barely touching, playing, teasing and taking her breath and her warmth in the tiniest increments he could handle.

When suddenly she pressed up onto her tiptoes, grabbed handfuls of his T-shirt and kissed him back.

Lights exploded behind his eyes as her soft warm body melted against him. Her mouth opened wide beneath his, welcoming him in. He'd made himself forget just how good this felt, as though remembering the taste and feel of her would mean he might not be able to give her up.

But, God, this was even better than everything he'd tried to forget. It was as though he could hear her very thoughts. He felt every emotion she had whirling inside her in that kiss— her anger at Felix, her frustration with herself, her confusion about how she felt about him, and how he felt about her.

She snuck a hand behind his head, changed angles and kissed him deeper, harder, more lushly. He almost lost complete control of himself then and there.

He wrapped his arms about her small form and lifted her off the ground. They tumbled onto her bed, legs intertwined, lips joined, hands grasping and clawing and trying to find skin where there was none to be found.

'Wait,' she called out and he all but leapt from on top of her.

The reprieve was like a life ring to a drowning man. He ran a fast hand through his thick hair, leaving it spiking in goodness knew how many directions.

Then he was forced to watch as she lifted her hips off the bed, slid the thick belt from her dress and threw it across the room before whipping her dress over her head, leaving herself naked, bar a pair of innocuous black underpants.

He barely had the chance to take his fill of her soft curves before she dragged him back into her arms.

But suddenly he was wearing far too many clothes.

He dragged his blazer from his back and whipped his T-shirt over his head between kisses. Her groans as he left her lips unattended were the most unendurable siren calls. But he knew this building tension, he knew her body so intimately, he knew it would all be worth it in the end.

He flipped onto his back, his fingers on the top button of his fly, when her hand stilled his progress.

The primal roar of defeat that built up inside him would have burst every window in the house.

Until her fingers peeled his back and took over. She was on her knees beside him, her breathing rate calm considering the circumstances, her dark eyes on the job at hand.

One button. His head fell back onto the bed.

A second button. He curled his fingernails into the bedspread.

The third button snapped and he jerked as the backs of her knuckles scraped against his erection.

She swung a leg over his thighs until her centre nestled against the bottom of his fly. She shifted closer, her legs spreading wider and her eyes turned to coal.

This is insane, he thought. *Pure sublime insanity*.

She leant forward, her small full breasts tipping forward, their pink peaks making his mouth water. Then her hand slid between his open fly and his cotton boxers and she cupped him as her teeth bit down on the softest part of his ear lobe.

He lasted about ten seconds before the fire inside him became too much. Even though he fought against the wrongness of what he was doing, he wasn't near ready for it to end. If they were going to do something foolish, they might as well do it right.

In one smooth move he tilted his ear out of reach of her

transcendent teeth, grabbed her blessed hand, lifted a knee between her thighs and rolled her onto her back.

Her adorable frown as she realised she'd been usurped was almost his undoing.

'Trust me,' he growled.

Time ticked by. Time in which he could have decided to be a better man and left her to get over him in peace.

But when her brow cleared, her eyes turned to molten gold, and she lifted her arms above her head in complete surrender, his position on the dark side was forever cemented.

He rid them both of the last of their clothes.

He slid her left knee to a right angle and pinned it to the bed with his leg, then set to teasing his tongue over every inch of her that had drawn his eye at any time since he'd first met her—the inside of her delicate wrists, the sexy dip above her clavicle, the tiny crease at the corner of her luscious lips.

He slowly drew her breast into his mouth. Then as she began to writhe beneath him his tongue circled her nipple. He didn't stop until she cried out from the pain of it.

Then when he knew she could stand it no longer, and with his leg still pressing hers apart, he cupped her.

He knew her so well. Every whimper, every flicker of pleasure lighting her golden eyes, every jerk beneath his hand. He knew her as if she'd been made to be pleasured by him and him alone.

The beauty and instinct of her response to him took him on the ride right along with her. Every whisper of heat that curled through her undulating body curled through him. Every catch of breath seared his own lungs. Every time their eyes connected he felt as if he knew her as well as he knew only himself.

His need soon became too great to ignore. He stroked his thumb against the perfect juncture between her legs and she bucked against him, grabbing his arms for support as she spilled apart beneath his touch.

But he didn't stop there. He couldn't. The moment her

breaths grew comfortable he brought her to the brink again. The look in her dark eyes as she clung to him was almost furious but at the same time she silently begged him to never stop.

When her own body gave way beneath the billows of pleasure, Dylan kissed her hard, drinking in her every breath, every moan until he was beyond ready for his own release.

How he'd managed to keep so long from doing so he had no idea. His patience, his absolute need to draw things out as long as he possibly could, even while he ached for her, while his erection remained strong and ready, was coming from somewhere other-worldly.

He glanced at his jeans. Too bloody far away. There was a condom in his wallet. He needed it now. But before he had the chance to tell her, she wrapped her legs about his hips and drew him in.

He slid inside her, a perfect fit. The sensation of skin on skin a phenomenon. The combination of friction and heat, and passion, and abandon and the wild, natural beauty of the woman in his arms took him somewhere he'd never been near before; she took him to the edge of heaven.

Clear, perfect, flawless, blameless, aspiring heaven.

And they made love as though they both knew it would be the last time. As if a lifetime's worth of pleasure had to be reaped from that one experience.

Dylan closed his eyes and tried not to imagine that he would never have an experience like it again. He let everything go bar the feel of her, the scent of her, the taste of her and finally, eventually, relief came.

Dylan woke up, stretched his arms over his head and opened his eyes. A wide-brimmed ceiling fan sent long shadows across a white ceiling. He was not in his own bed.

He glanced sideways to face a curtain of silky dark hair splayed across a white pillow and a pale naked back glowing in the moonlight.

Wynnie….

He reached out to run his hand down her beautiful back, then stopped himself just in time. Making love to her had been selfish enough, prolonging any kind of connection would be plain cruel.

He pushed the sheet aside, slid from the bed, stepped into his jeans and collected the rest of his clothes before padding silently from the room.

He stopped at the doorway, allowing himself one last glance. She looked so young, so fresh, so unsullied. He'd always thought himself a cut above his whole life. A Kelly with the privilege, smarts, sense and pride that came with it. But looking at that peaceful face he knew Wynnie deserved far better than him.

He moved into the kitchen and finished dressing. And that was when he saw the postcard that had set this unexpected night in motion propped on the bench by a bowl of loose change.

So innocuous looking. So tactless.

If Jack ever did track her brother down he'd ring the kid's skinny neck for what he'd done to his sister. Not just the once but over and over again for every time he reached out, yet gave her nothing real to hold on to.

Dylan grabbed the postcard, found a pen, turned over the card to its blank white back and did what the kid ought to have done himself.

He wrote: 'Sun's shining. Having a blast. Wish you were here.'

Once it was too late to take them back, he ran his thumb over the words, hoping she would never guess that, for the five seconds he had taken to write them, the words could well have come from him.

He propped the postcard writing side out where she'd left it and he walked out of her cottage and out of her life just as he'd warned her he would.

Dylan shoved his hands in the pockets of his jeans, and

turned the collar of his jacket up to stave off the cool night air as he jogged out to his car.

That was it. Enough was enough. The time had come for him to snap back into focus and get on with the life he'd known before she came along.

Because the corner he'd backed himself into—the titanic responsibility of protecting his prodigious family from every kind of harm, no matter what he might have to sacrifice in order to do so—was so large a part of who he now was, going back there was all he knew how to do.

Wynnie trudged into the office late Friday morning, feeling like a wrung-out rag.

The postcard, half a bottle of wine, half a tub of ice cream, Dylan, the postcard… How she managed to get out of bed at all was a testament to her dedication to her work.

She pushed her sunglasses higher onto her nose to cut out the glare of the overhead lights and wondered how on earth she could stand going another round of phone calls to CEOs and managing directors who didn't want to give her the time of day.

Dedication, schmedication. After she checked her messages she was going to take a sickie and that was that.

Because last night… She'd shown Dylan exactly how she felt about him. She knew he'd seen she was in deep, and that was why he'd stayed. He'd all but told her he wasn't in the same place, and that was why he'd left.

Still, when she'd seen the fresh handwriting on the postcard her heart had leapt. Till she had realised his sweet words had been his way of telling her he knew why she'd been so steadfast with Felix even though the kid didn't know it himself.

Family first, that was what he'd been telling her. For her. And for him. It had been his way of setting her free.

And now her heart felt as if it had been bruised, stung, poisoned and flicked with sharp fingernails. It seemed she'd never learn.

She turned the corner into her office and was met with a
standing ovation from all the staff. She stumbled backwards,
knocking over a potted mulberry plant and losing her sunglasses down her top.

Once she'd righted herself she looked over her shoulder to
see what she was missing.

Hannah stepped forwards from the crowd. 'Where the hell
have you been?' she whispered through a massive toothy smile.

'Errands,' Wynnie said, rather than, *I slept through my alarm
because I was up much of the night having hot break-up sex
with a possible client of ours who I was never really going out
with even though I'm fairly sure that I am actually crazy in love
with.* 'Do you want to tell me what on earth's going on?'

'It's been one hell of a morning. Faxes, e-mails, the phones
have been ringing off the hook.'

'And…?'

Hannah stepped back, spread her arms at Wynnie as if she
were the prize on a game show and shouted, 'And Eric Carlisle
from the Kelly Investment Group just rang to say that all
terms proposed by you have been agreed to and that he will
be the new point man on the CFC/KInG joint venture.'

The office went crazy once more, this time throwing
confetti at her made of crushed two-minute noodles they'd
probably found in the staff kitchen. When champagne corks
started popping Wynnie ducked her head and made a beeline
for the washroom.

She wrapped her hands around the edge of the cold sink
and waited until her heavy breathing settled into a non-
fainting type rhythm. Then she let go, and pulled her hair off
her face and looked at herself in the mirror.

Somehow she looked just fine. Her hair was neat and
bouncing. Her make-up was flawless. Her deep purple velvet
top with its plunging neckline, and her skin-tight, pre-loved
designer jeans were just saucy enough for her workmates to
shake their heads and think, *Wow, weren't we clever to hire*

this spitfire. She didn't look as though she'd been to hell, and heaven and back again in the past twenty-four hours.

She was so damned good at her job of making people think what she wanted them to think nobody even knew when she was a raging mess.

Nobody except Dylan. Barely three words into the phone call and he'd known.

The washroom door swung inwards, and Hannah's head popped through. 'Sweetie. Whatcha doing in here?'

She squinted at her picture-perfect reflection in the mirror. 'It's a really long story.'

Hannah shut the door behind her and locked it. 'The champagne's a-flowing. They won't even notice we're gone. I've got time.'

Wynnie turned and leant her backside against the sink. And she filled Hannah in on the briefest update possible. Leaving out certain things. Leaving out Felix and his postcard, and Dylan and his succubus. She found she couldn't find the words to talk to Hannah about her family, even though she'd lived through the worst of it with her. Yet last night, with Dylan, the words had spilled out so easily she'd wondered how she'd ever found it hard before.

'Sheesh,' Hannah said.

'I know, right? And right now, I've just been given what I wanted all along—the biggest client the CFC could have landed. And it was all my doing. I should have been doing cart-wheels and demanding high fives of everyone in the office.'

'But not so much?'

'Not so much.'

Wynnie looked down at the pointy toes of her shoes. Actually she felt a lot like crying. Again. 'I didn't earn it. He's given it to me as a consolation prize.'

It was Dylan's way of saying thanks but no thanks, only this time not to her proposal but to her.

'I'm such an idiot.'

'You're a trouper.'

'And you know what? I'm angry! For him to do it this way, and through Eric... If there weren't so many other people involved with the deal, and if the outcome wasn't so bloody fantastic, I'd rip the contract up and eat it piece by piece while standing in front of his bloody building.'

'Don't be ridiculous. You'd recycle the paper it was printed on.' Hannah moved over and leant on the sink next to hers. 'I did try to warn you, hon. He's a hard man from a hard family. And you are so very, very soft.'

That was just it. His family was lovely. And he was kind, and gentle and caring. Or maybe it was exactly as Hannah said and she was just too soft to assume the worst. Always had been. Always would.

Wynnie leant her heavy head on her friend's shoulder. 'I think I deserve a long weekend.'

'I think so, too.' Hannah gave her a nudge with her hip. 'Go. Right out the front door now. And don't come back till like Wednesday. I'll cover for you.'

Wynnie gave her a quick kiss on the cheek, grabbed her purse and fled before she changed her mind.

As she hit the pavement outside the building, warm spring sunshine beating down on her face, she wondered if Dylan had any idea the good he'd done by approving the deal. Not for her, but for the city. She doubted it. So much she wanted to ring him and blast him and tell him off and applaud him and kiss him all at the same time.

Argh, he was so frustrating! Even now, even after it was all said and done. He was one great hulking clueless walking contradiction. And *that* was why she loved him.

He was beautiful; he was challenging. But most of all she loved him for his principles. She loved him because of the strength of his loyalty to those he loved. He was everything she hoped she could be.

He just refused to see it.

But she couldn't tell him. The deal was now in the hands of the CFC ground crews, and Eric. And she knew that this time he wouldn't take her call.

Wynnie was so mentally, emotionally and physically exhausted she slept all Friday afternoon, and most of the day Saturday, feeling as if jet lag had finally hit.

Then bright and early Sunday morning, she got a phone call that woke her up better than a bucket of iced water over the head.

On Sunday morning Dylan sat slumped in his office chair staring out of his large window, looking past the view of South Bank and out into nothingness.

He still wore the same clothes from the day before. His head felt as if a jackhammer had taken up residence inside it, and with Eric not about he had to make his own coffee, the one life skill he readily admitted he sucked at.

His office phone rang.

As he had every time the phone had rung the past couple of days, for a moment he imagined it would be *her*—wanting him, needing him, gently urging him to be a better man.

The very thought of her made him feel tight and loose and wasted. But that was too bad. She was a smart woman, he had no doubt that she knew that postcard was his last hurrah. She wouldn't be calling him again.

By putting Eric in charge of the CFC deal, he'd made damn sure he'd left no avenue for her to even try.

The phone rang again. Loudly. He spun on his chair, flipped it from the cradle and yelled, 'What?'

'Kelly, it's Garry Sloane. Of the Allied Press Corps.'

Dylan gripped the phone tighter. As if he didn't know the exact tones of the scum-sucking cretin who'd been the first to spill his worst day all over the Sunday papers years before.

It was the one downside of his job, that he had to play nice with the sod. Strangling a journalist with his own computer keyboard cord would make it a tad difficult to remain the head of Media Relations.

'Sloane,' he growled, relishing the fact there was someone in the world he disliked more than he currently disliked himself. 'I must have missed the roses and chocolates you sent in apology for assaulting me last weekend.'

'Yeah,' he shot back. 'They're in the mail.'

'What do you want?'

'I'm running a story tomorrow I thought you might like to comment on.'

'Go on.'

'It's not a new story as such, more like a "where are they now" piece. It's about a woman called Guinevere Lambert who got herself into a bit of trouble with the law several years back, and has now suddenly become one of our fair city's favourite daughters. You might know her better as Wynnie Devereaux.'

Dylan shot his chair upright and slammed his fist on his desk so hard his coffee mug jumped and slid off the edge, landing on the carpeted floor with a pathetic thud.

'Shall I continue?' Sloane asked.

'Not over the phone,' Dylan said, his mind whirring a million miles a minute. He shot a look at his watch. 'Meet me at my place in say…three hours. Until then don't call another living soul about this piece.'

'You'd better have something good.'

'You'd better hope I don't slap you with a lawsuit the size of my bank account for the pain and suffering of my split lip.'

'Three hours,' Sloane said.

Then Dylan slammed the phone down so hard it snapped in two.

CHAPTER TWELVE

ON MONDAY morning, when she ought to have been getting ready for work, Wynnie instead sat on her back deck, sipping from a cooling cup of green tea and staring out through the palm fronds filling her small leafy backyard.

The sun was shining, the sky was cerulean blue, a light breeze picked up the scents of the myriad spring flowers dotting the undulating hills around her Spring Hill abode.

This was Brisbane at its best. Something she'd only experienced for about nine months in her late teens before Felix had fallen and her whole life had been whipped out from under her.

The 'beautiful one day, perfect the next' nature of the place hadn't been enough to salve her heart then, and so far it wasn't doing all that much to salve it now.

Knowing she couldn't put off the inevitable for much longer, she moved her glass of orange juice off the top of the folded newspaper, not caring that condensation had left a wet dark ring over the sports section.

She slowly opened it up, her fingers shaking as she turned to the front page, ready to slowly flick through until she found her photograph, her true story, her ticket to unemployment and ridicule and humiliation.

Her hands shook and she kept the paper closed a minute longer. She squeezed her eyes shut, took several deep breaths and tried to meditate her way to a happy place.

When the happiest place she could think of was being wrapped naked in Dylan's strong arms, it didn't help her heart rate settle in the least. Her muscles tensed, her nerves twitched, her skin began to overheat.

Her eyes flew open and she pinched herself on the back of the hand. *Enough.* If she was that worked up before she read the article she might as well knock herself out now.

She gripped the newspaper in both hands.

When Sloane had called, looking for information about her past, she'd told him to go bite himself. Then after pacing the house for twenty minutes she'd called her bosses at the CFC and told them everything, offering her resignation. She'd then called a female reporter who she'd built a relationship with since the handcuff stunt and given her the exclusive.

For the time had come to stop running—from her past, and from her desires. She wasn't Felix. She would never hurt others in the pursuit of getting what she wanted. She was a helper. She was a guardian angel for the planet. But she was also a woman with needs that deserved to be fulfilled without constant concern that an incident in her distant past could ruin it all.

She took a deep breath, opened the paper…

And didn't get past the front page.

She leapt off her chair and stood staring at the headline. Above a photograph of Quinn Kelly it read: The King is Dying, Long Live the KInG.

She sped-read the article so fast she got whiplash.

Quinn, Dylan's gorgeous father, had major heart problems, had suffered two heart attacks in recent months, he no longer ran the family business as everyone thought he did, all of which the family had kept under close wraps. Until now…

The timing rang a bell inside her head. But she had to keep reading. She had to know everything.

A full-page story on the front led to several more inside, all about Quinn's failing health. She held a hand to her heart as she read that he was doing as well as could be expected, but had already taken a large step back in the business and would be retiring as of that day. Brendan had been secretly running the empire for months. There was a special interest piece from Mary Kelly's point of view with a photo of her whole beautiful family that must have been taken recently as Cameron's new wife was in the shot.

But what caught at her most was quote after quote from Dylan. His name was mentioned so many times she wondered if he'd written the article himself. She checked the byline.

Her backside slumped onto the chair so hard she bruised.

'Garry Sloane?' she read aloud in case she was imagining it.

And then everything came together as if a hurricane had passed and she were left surveying the damage in its wake.

She hadn't been the only one with a secret. Hers had been about to be revealed. Sloane was such a sleaze he must have called Dylan after she'd told him where to go. And Dylan had somehow, for some reason, chosen to sacrifice his own intensely held privacy in order to keep hers safe.

To keep *her* safe.

She leapt off the chair and ran inside, grabbed her house keys, realised she was wearing sheer pyjamas and a see-through robe and ran back into her bedroom.

She stripped off her pants, threw a navy velvet jacket over her lacy pyjama top, tugged on jeans hanging over the back of a cane chair, and slid her feet into her handiest shoes which happened to be red high heels.

Whipping her hair from its scrunchy and slapping some sunscreen onto her cheeks, she scooted out to the deck, grabbed the paper, checked she hadn't been imagining the whole thing and then took off out of the front door.

It wasn't yet seven in the morning.

Monday? Yep, Monday.

She knew exactly where the great hulking fool would be.

Dylan stood in line to buy his own double-strength white chocolate mocha with extra cinnamon. It was almost enough for him to rescind Eric's promotion and get the kid back to do his grunt work.

The café door swung open, and something made Dylan turn. Whether it was the shift of chocolate-brown hair on the edge of his vision, the stirring of sexual tension in the air, or just plain instinct, he found himself looking into Wynnie's big beautiful brown eyes.

She stood in the entrance, brandishing what looked like a third of a scrunched newspaper as though she might slap him over the back of the head with it the first chance she had.

And he knew why.

With his father's news out there, he was sure he'd hear from her in the next few days. Or that evening. Or before lunch. Actually if she hadn't called within the next two hours he was going to turn up on her doorstep with a chai latté and a pair of cream buns.

'Wynnie,' he said, his voice as cool as he could hope for it to be considering two steps would put her within touching distance. And that was a mile closer than he'd thought he'd ever get to her again. To that luscious skin, those edible lips, this woman.

'Don't you Wynnie me,' she said, her voice coming to him as though she'd swallowed sandpaper.

He stepped out of line and weaved through the small, and extremely attentive, crowd to manoeuvre her out of the way. 'Well, now I'm confused,' he said with as disarming a smile as he could muster. 'Which name would you prefer I use?'

Her face was livid. Her chest rising and falling. Her hair a shaggy mess. Her eyes wild. He'd never been as turned on in his entire life.

'Stop changing the subject,' she hissed. 'What have you gone and done?'

Their fan club was growing by the second. One young guy even lifted his mobile phone, which gave off the distant click of a photo being taken. Dylan glanced around for an alternative exit, when the girl behind the counter caught his eye, madly waving at him as she was.

She cocked her head to his left, and mouthed, 'Back door.'

He gave her a nod. She smiled and shrugged. And he reminded himself to tip her everything in his wallet the next time he came in.

When Wynnie opened her mouth to rant anew, he grabbed her by the upper arm and half pushed, half dragged her through the crowd, down a small hall, past the kitchen and out of the back door.

A small, hopelessly untended garden stopped sharply at a cliff's edge. Dylan took them down a series of old stone steps until he and Wynnie stood on a secluded jetty jutting out into the Morningside stretch of the Brisbane River. Tall reeds and weeping willows created privacy, a thick fall of jacaranda flowers carpeted the wooden jetty at their feet, and sunshine blasting through thick tufts of flowering yellow wattle leant a strange golden glow over everything.

'Now,' he said, 'what was it you were trying to say?'

She threw the newspaper at him and it scattered to the soft purple ground in slowly wafting pieces. 'Your father is really sick.'

'I know.'

Her face softened. 'I'm so sorry. Please tell your mum if there's anything I can do, I'll do it.'

'Thank you.'

She looked from one eye to the other, the strength of her feelings for him seeping from her very skin. And instead of feeling trapped, or suspicious, or terrified, or unworthy, finally it just felt right.

Then she reached out and slapped him hard on the arm.
'Ow!'

'Oh, shut up. Don't you think I know what you did? Don't you think Garry Bloody Sloane called me first?'

She pushed away from him, paced a step till she hit the water's edge, then spun back. A shaft of sunlight split the glade, lighting on her alone. She appeared to be naked beneath her jacket bar some tiny pieces of lace that flashed at her stomach when she moved. All it seemed he'd have to do was flick open that one button at her waist and all would be revealed. The bruise forming on his arm told him the time was not yet right for such a move. The thickening of his blood told him the time was coming.

'You've kept your father's health concerns private for a very good reason,' she continued, 'so that he has the space to stay healthy. I've kept mum about my past because I feel humiliated that I didn't spend enough time with my own flesh and blood to see the bad coming and people were hurt.'

'People would have been hurt if we didn't tell the truth soon, too.'

'People,' she repeated, again looking deep into his eyes. 'What people?'

'Friends, colleagues, investors, the business itself. It was the right thing to do.'

'And yesterday. You tell me, and I want to hear it from your lips, why suddenly yesterday?'

'You were right,' he said, sliding his hands into the pockets of his black suit trousers so that he could get through this part without touching her, holding her, kissing her. There were things that had to be said first. 'Sloane called me yesterday morning. He told me what he was planning to write about you and he wanted my input.'

She looked so worried, as if maybe she was putting herself on the line for him again, and he was going to let her down again. As if she believed in him so much it physically hurt her to think she could be wrong about him still. He'd never wanted to hold her so much.

'All I knew was that I had to do everything in my considerable power to make sure he didn't do it.'

'Why?'

Hell, had his stubbornness wounded her that badly?

He took a step towards her. 'Wynnie, honey, you know why. You've known why far longer than I have. I did it because you are braver and stronger and far more honest than I will ever be.'

She swallowed hard.

He reached out and took her arm. She didn't flinch. She didn't pull away. He took her other arm, and though it was physically nearly impossible, he left enough space between them for her to breathe.

'I called a family meeting yesterday afternoon,' he said. 'I told them I had accepted your proposal on behalf of KInG as it was smart and necessary and up until that moment I had been acting like a horse's ass. I also told them that the time had come for all of us to stop hiding behind the walls of Kelly Manor and to come clean. If we were going to move forward, as a business, and as a family, we needed to unburden ourselves of everything holding us back.'

'You said all that?'

He took a small step closer. She had to tilt her head to look him in the eye. Her exposed neck was almost too much temptation. Almost. He knew there was better yet to come.

'I told them all that, and I could feel the relief sweep through the room. As it turns out I can be rather persistent when I want to be and since damage control is my area they've agreed to keep mum for my sake all this time.'

'So it's all okay? With your family, I mean? They're not angry with you?'

'It's better than okay. Because I also told them that I hadn't come to that conclusion lightly. I told them that Garry Sloane, of all people, had forced me to prioritise my life in a split second. And it had been so easy it was ridiculous.'

He made sure he had a good grip. He'd had time to process all of this. Still his voice was very slightly shaky as he said, 'I told my family that I realised in that split second that I had met the woman I wanted to spend the rest of my life with. That I would do whatever it took to make her see that, despite the many things I had done in a foolish effort to prove otherwise, I am the man she thought I was. I told them that woman was you.'

He was glad he'd held her tight as her knees gave way. He hauled her into his arms. Her hands rested on his shoulders so that the length of her was pressed against the length of him. Now he was ready to get to the good part.

'Wynnie Devereaux,' he said, 'I am in love with you. I think I have been in love with you since the moment I saw you hooked up to that ridiculous sculpture, smiling, laughing, trying your dandiest to look comfortable while nickel burnt your wrists.'

Tears filled her eyes as if she'd turned on an inner faucet. As he always had the moment those eyes of hers gleamed, he went into protector mode. His hands cupped her face, as gently as possible.

'You love me?' she said on a gulp.

'I do love you. So deeply it hurts. But the hurt is so far overshadowed by the good I barely notice it.'

She put a hand over his and leant into his palm. 'I love you, too.'

He nodded. 'I know you do, beautiful girl. I know you do.'

She smiled, radiantly, and the brightest of lights burst inside him, filling him with so much pleasure, so much happiness he wasn't sure he'd ever know what to do with it.

'Now back to that statue,' he said. 'I've been thinking all morning about tearing the thing down so I can mount it in our front yard. It would be the kind of talking piece the neighbours would hate.'

'*Our* front yard?' she repeated.

For the first time since she'd come looking for him, Dylan faltered. Not having ever been in this exact place before, where he knew his heart was on the line and he was deliberately putting it there anyway, he wasn't sure if he was moving too fast. Or if it was even possible to move too fast.

He slid his hand into the back of her hair, and let her see the full truth of his feelings. 'I'm not sure the CFC would approve of you sticking it up in front of their cottage. And my place has so much room.'

'How many rooms?' she asked, her cheek lifting into a soft, sexy smile that slid through him like molten lava.

He wrapped an arm tighter about her waist and pulled her closer. Her head lolled back and her breath released on a sigh. His body temperature went up two degrees.

'Too many,' he rasped. 'But there's only one you need to familiarise yourself with for starters.'

She slunk closer still, her knee sliding between his, her breasts pressing in against his chest until he was certain she wasn't wearing a bra. 'If you say the kitchen we have issues, my friend.'

He raised an eyebrow. 'There is a perfectly good bench in the kitchen, which might serve our purpose one day. But for starters I thought we might try out the bed in my room. I had the mattress shipped over from the Four Seasons in Paris. You have never felt anything like it.'

'Your room?'

He wet his suddenly dry lips. 'If you're game, how about we go ahead and make it our room?'

'Our room. I don't think you have any idea how much I love the sound of that.'

'Yeah,' he said, nudging her nose with his. 'I think I do.'

She tilted her head, he tilted his and they kissed. Slow, sensuous, disarming.

Being that they were them it soon dissolved into something hotter, harder, deeper. Dylan slid his hand between them, unbuttoned her jacket and groaned as his hand closed over her breast. If any boats had chosen to sail on past at that moment they would have been in for quite a show.

Wynnie pulled gently away and said, 'Now this all works out just beautifully for me, you know, considering I'm probably about to lose my job, and therefore my house.'

He slid his hand down her back to cup her buttocks, pressing her against his rising hardness. She didn't seem to notice. His beautiful tease.

But then she pushed away far enough that she could look him directly in the eyes, and so that she could make sure he was doing the same. 'In the spirit of full disclosure—'

'You were once a man and your real name is Kevin. I knew there was a reason why you didn't throw yourself at me the moment I unshackled you and your hands were free.'

She held her hand over his mouth, and he was hard pressed not to nibble at her fingers. To slide them into his mouth and scrape his teeth along each and every one.

'While you were giving your story to Sloane, I gave my story to another reporter. It had obviously been usurped by more pressing news. But it will come out.'

By the look in her eyes it was as though she thought that would make a lick of difference to him. Newfound strength made him stand up straighter as he planned on spending his life making sure she felt secure every day of hers.

'Sweetheart, it's time you realise that all you did was stand up for the brother you loved. The CFC are far too smart a bunch of people to let you go for something that was never your fault. And as for me, if that's as dark as your secrets get then I'm hoping we can hurry up and start to forge some much darker ones of our own.'

He buried his nose in her hair. Her fingers gripped his shoulders hard. And he knew without a doubt that the best sex of his life, and hers, was yet to come.

'I read the paper and I came straight here,' she said, trying with all her might to find her way back to the subject. 'I haven't even showered.'

'You smell great.' Boy, did she smell great. Like cotton sheets, and spring flowers. So great he kissed her neck, and gave it a soft lick. God help him, she tasted even better au natural.

'Your family—'

'Aren't anywhere near here, thank God,' he said, moving to stoke gentle kisses along her décolletage.

'But they are so important to you and—'

'And what?'

'And me.'

He pulled back so that he could look right into her beautiful brown eyes.

When he'd told them about how he felt for Wynnie they'd reacted with tears, hugs, phone calls to distant relatives, wiped brows, bets paid out, and wedding plans begun. Dylan thought it best to ease Wynnie into the hard, fast, no-holds-barred Kelly way of doing things. Now he'd enchanted her he wasn't going to do anything to make her wish otherwise.

'Brendan wants to hire you,' he said. 'Dad wants to adopt you. Mum wants to introduce you to everybody. Meg wants to know where you get your clothes. Cameron is pretty much still in a newlywed haze so might not even remember he's met you before, but the odds are in your favour.'

'I wish Felix was around so you could meet him. You'd drive one another crazy and it would be so much fun to watch.'

Dylan lifted his head and looked into her eyes, knowing that he couldn't miss the chance at seeing again the love she had therein, even if this one time it wasn't directed at him.

'I had planned to save this bit for later…'

'What bit?'

'I might have a small addendum to add to your reporter friend's story.'

Wynnie's brow furrowed and he could feel the deepening

of her breaths through his chest. Her hand gripped his shirt tight, and she nodded, just the once. 'Tell me.'

'I've had conversations with a colleague of mine in the federal prosecutor's office about Felix's case. Over time, after tracking down several others involved in the caper, they downgraded his charge to an accessory. They have known for some time that he was a wide-eyed kid roped in at the last minute and that he had no say in the planning, and little in the execution, bar being a lookout.'

Her spare hand slapped over her mouth and tears welled in her eyes.

Dylan held her tight for the next part. 'My friend agreed that if he comes back to town and turns himself in, he will be charged as a minor, given probation and his records will be sealed.'

'He'll be free?'

'Wynnie, I'm hoping you'll both be free.'

'But we don't even know where—'

'Jack, my investigator mate, found him. He's spoken to him. Felix knows the deal. He's on a plane as we speak. He'll be here tomorrow.'

The tears that had threatened to spill were suddenly gone. In their place, radiance. Pure unadulterated sunshine, and this time it was all for him.

She slid a hand through the hair above his ear, and he breathed in deep.

'I told you that you were a good man,' she said.

'Yeah, you did. And for some silly reason I've begun to believe it.'

'How can I ever repay you?'

'My gorgeous girl, you'll never, ever have the need.'

He leant in to kiss her and she pressed a hand to his chest. He rolled his eyes and growled at the sky. 'What does a guy have to do to get some appreciation around here?'

Her voice shook with laughter as she said, 'I was just about to thank you for signing KInG on with the CFC.'

'Actions not words are the way to thank a man for such a thing.' He nipped at her ear lobe and she shivered.

'And why is Eric the contact at KInG?'

'Did I know you could talk this much?'

'You did, you just love me so much you forgot.'

'Hopefully we can continue in that vein.'

'So why Eric…?'

Dylan let Wynnie go. Holding her so close but not getting any closer was pure agony. He took a step back and held an arm between them when she stepped his way. 'Now you've closed the deal will you be the contact at the CFC?'

'If they let me keep my job, then still no. My job's to ring 'em in. It's someone else's job to follow through.'

'Well, that was the first reason. The second reason is that Eric called me a cretin.'

She took another step towards him, her shoes crunching in the purple flowers. His hand landed upon her waist. She slid until his hands slunk beneath her jacket, opening it to reveal the sheer lace top, and the naked gorgeousness beneath.

'He said that to your face?' she asked.

'To my face,' he growled.

'Why? I mean, not why did he say it to your face, but which of the thousand asinine things you do each day finally made him crack?'

He dragged his eyes from her beautiful torso to look her in the eye. 'I let you go.'

The sass dissolved into sweetness as she said, 'Oh.'

And if possible he loved her all the more.

'Mmm. So I fired him as my assistant and moved him into development. More money. More autonomy. He sent me flowers. Crazy kid.'

'Not so crazy,' she said, her voice a husky whisper as his thumb grazed the edge of her breast.

As her body grew pliant and soft he slid his hand around her back, drew her close and let himself just revel in the fact that this woman had come bursting into his inert world, clearing the mist from his eyes, showing him how to breathe deep of life, and now he would get to touch her like this, feel her, be near her, joke with her, kiss her, make her melt as long as he remained smart enough to realise what he had.

His last secret was that he hoped that would be for the rest of his days.

Wynnie blinked up at him, then into the bright sunlight. Her brow furrowed and she glanced down at the purple flowers sticking to their shoes, and through the bright yellow wattle and across the river, and only just seemed to realise where they were. 'Now how on earth did we end up—?'

Dylan silenced her with another kiss. The kind of hard, fast, thorough kiss that ought to give her something else to think about for a few minutes.

When he pulled away it took her a few moments to open her eyes. They fluttered up at him, all liquid and dreamy.

He loved this woman. He loved her vivacity, her bravery, her impudence. It was so obvious, now the light had been switched on he knew it would never turn off again.

'This spot is so romantic,' she said, her voice husky as all get out. 'Who knew you had it in you?'

'Complete accident, so don't get any ideas that I'm the romantic type.'

She held a hand to her heart. 'I'm shocked to hear it.'

His cheeks warmed. He could actually feel them turning pink. What other changes could this woman possibly bring to his life? If he started singing Pavarotti songs in the shower that was the end of him.

He cupped her cheek, and looked into those eyes that always told him so much. 'But in a funny kind of way telling my family's story was my version of a love letter to you.'

'On the front page of the paper?'

He grinned. 'I'm a Kelly. I don't know any other way.'

Wynnie slid a hand through his hair, making a mess of the slick 'do. 'I do love you, Dylan Kelly. And not because you stood up for me, but because I always knew you would.'

'Even though I'm insular, jaded, a workaholic, am ruthless and self-serving?'

'Save that for the paying public,' she scoffed. 'You are a marshmallow. My marshmallow. My beautiful, generous, big-hearted, loyal marshmallow.'

Every word out of her mouth sank in and stuck until he began to really believe she was right.

He held her chin between his finger and thumb and waited until she was looking him in the eye. 'You once said to me that if one person can make a difference, a hundred people can change the world.'

'That sounds like something I'd say.'

'Well, I'm thinking perhaps you underestimated people.'

'I did?'

'Mmm. There's only one of you and yet you managed to change my world all on your own.'

He pulled her to him, or maybe she leant towards him. Either way, they kissed. It was beautiful. It was melting hot.

And Wynnie was not the only one to take a sickie that day.

* * * * *

The debt, the payment, the price!

A ruthless ruler and his virgin queen. Trembling with
the fragility of new spring buds, Ionanthe will go to her
husband. She was given as penance, but he'll take her
for pleasure!

*Harlequin Presents® is delighted to unveil an exclusive
extract from Penny Jordan's new book
A BRIDE FOR HIS MAJESTY'S PLEASURE*

PEOPLE WERE PRESSING in on her—the crowd was carrying her along with it, almost causing her to lose her balance. Fear stabbed through Ionanthe as she realized how vulnerable she was.

An elderly man grabbed her arm, warning her, 'You had better do better by our prince than that sister of yours. She shamed us all when she shamed him.'

Spittle flecked his lips, and his eyes were wild with anger as he shook her arm painfully. The people surrounding her who had been smiling before were now starting to frown, their mood changing. She looked around for the guards, but couldn't see any of them. She was alone in a crowd that was quickly becoming hostile to her. She hadn't thought it was in her nature to panic, but she was beginning to do so now.

Then Ionanthe felt another hand on her arm, in a touch that extraordinarily her body somehow recognized. And a familiar voice was saying firmly, 'Princess Ionanthe has already paid the debt owed by her family to the people of Fortenegro. Her presence here today as my bride and your princess is proof of that.'

He was at her side now, his presence calming the crowd

and forcing the old man to release her as the crowd began to murmur their agreement to his words.

Calmly but determinedly Max was guiding her back through the crowd. A male voice called out to him from the crowd. 'Make sure you get us a fine future prince on her as soon as may be, Your Highness.'

The sentiment was quickly taken up by others, who threw in their own words of bawdy advice to the new bridegroom. Ionanthe fought to stop her face from burning with angry humiliated color. Torn between unwanted relief that she had been rescued and discomfort about what was being said, Ionanthe took refuge in silence as they made their way back toward the palace.

They had almost reached the main entrance when once again Max told hold of her arm. This time she fought her body's treacherous reaction, clamping down on the sensation that shot through her veins and stiffening herself against it. The comments she had been subjected to had brought home to her the reality of what she had done; they clung inside her head, rubbing as abrasively against her mind as burrs would have rubbed against her skin.

'Isn't it enough for you to have forced me into marrying you? Must you force me to obey your will physically, as well?' she challenged him bitterly.

Max felt the forceful surge of his own anger swelling through him to meet her biting contempt, shocking him with its intensity as he fought to subdue it.

Not once during the months he had been married to Eloise had she ever come anywhere near arousing him emotionally the way that Ionanthe could, despite the fact that he had known her only a matter of days. She seemed to delight in pushing him—punishing him for their current situation, no doubt, he reminded himself as his anger subsided. It was completely out of character for him to let anyone get under his skin enough to make him react emotionally when his response should be purely cerebral.

'Far from wishing to force you to do anything, I merely wanted to suggest that we use the side entrance to the palace. That way we will attract less attention.'

He had a point, Ionanthe admitted grudgingly, but she wasn't going to say so. Instead she started to walk toward the door set in one of the original castle towers, both of them slipping through the shadows the building now threw across the square, hidden from the view of the people crowding the palace steps. She welcomed the peace of its stone interior after the busyness of the square. Her dress had become uncomfortably heavy and her head had started to ache. The reality of what she had done had begun to set in, filling her with a mixture of despair and panic. But she mustn't think of herself and her immediate future, she told herself as she started to climb the stone steps that she knew from memory led to a corridor that connected the old castle to the more modern palace.

She had almost reached the last step when somehow or other she stepped on the hem of her gown, the accidental movement unbalancing her and causing her to stumble. Max, who was several steps below her, heard the small startled sound she made and raced up the stairs, catching her as she fell.

If she was trembling with the fragility of new spring buds in the wind, then it was because of her shock. If she felt weak and her heart was pounding with dangerous speed, then it was because of the weight of her gown. If she couldn't move, then it was because of the arms that imprisoned her.

She had to make him release her. It was dangerous to be in his arms. She looked up at him, her gaze traveling the distance from his chin to his mouth and then refusing to move any farther. What had been a mere tremor of shock had now become a fiercely violent shudder that came from deep within her and ached through her. She felt dizzy, light-headed, removed from everything about herself she considered 'normal' to become, instead, a woman who hungered for something unknown and forbidden.

* * * * *

Give yourself a present this Christmas—
pick up a copy of
A BRIDE FOR HIS MAJESTY'S PLEASURE
by Penny Jordan,
available December 2009
from Harlequin Presents®!

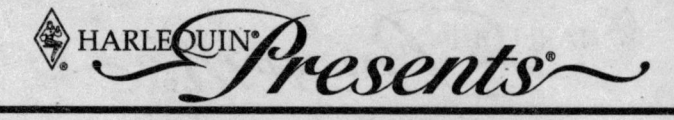

HARLEQUIN *Presents*

TWO CROWNS, TWO ISLANDS, ONE LEGACY

A royal family torn apart by pride and its lust for power, reunited by purity and passion

THE ROYAL HOUSE *of* KAREDES

Harlequin Presents is proud to bring you
the last three installments from
The Royal House of Karedes.
You won't want to miss out!

THE FUTURE KING'S LOVE-CHILD
by Melanie Milburne, December 2009

RUTHLESS BOSS, ROYAL MISTRESS
by Natalie Anderson, January 2010

THE DESERT KING'S HOUSEKEEPER BRIDE
by Carol Marinelli, February 2010

INNOCENT WIVES

Powerful men—ready to wed!

They're passionate, persuasive and don't
play by the rules…they make them!

And now they need brides.

But when their innocent wives say "I Do," can it ever
be more than a marriage in name only?

Look out for all our exciting books this month:

Powerful Greek, Unworldly Wife #81
by SARAH MORGAN

Ruthlessly Bedded, Forcibly Wedded #82
by ABBY GREEN

Blackmailed Bride, Inexperienced Wife #83
by ANNIE WEST

The British Billionaire's Innocent Bride #84
by SUSANNE JAMES

www.eHarlequin.com

HPE1209

REQUEST YOUR FREE BOOKS!

HARLEQUIN *Presents* ®

PASSION
GUARANTEED
SEDUCTION

2 FREE NOVELS
PLUS 2
FREE GIFTS!

YES! Please send me 2 FREE Harlequin Presents® novels and my 2 FREE gifts (gifts are worth about $10). After receiving them, if I don't wish to receive any more books, I can return the shipping statement marked "cancel". If I don't cancel, I will receive 6 brand-new novels every month and be billed just $4.05 per book in the U.S. or $4.74 per book in Canada. That's a savings of close to 15% off the cover price! It's quite a bargain! Shipping and handling is just 50¢ per book*. I understand that accepting the 2 free books and gifts places me under no obligation to buy anything. I can always return a shipment and cancel at any time. Even if I never buy another book, the two free books and gifts are mine to keep forever.   106 HDN EYRQ 306 HDN EYR2

Name	(PLEASE PRINT)
Address	Apt. #
City	State/Prov.	Zip/Postal Code

Signature (if under 18, a parent or guardian must sign)

Mail to the Harlequin Reader Service:
IN U.S.A.: P.O. Box 1867, Buffalo, NY 14240-1867
IN CANADA: P.O. Box 609, Fort Erie, Ontario L2A 5X3

Not valid to current subscribers of Harlequin Presents books.

Are you a current subscriber of Harlequin Presents books and want to receive the larger-print edition? Call 1-800-873-8635 today!

* Terms and prices subject to change without notice. Prices do not include applicable taxes. Sales tax applicable in N.Y. Canadian residents will be charged applicable provincial taxes and GST. Offer not valid in Quebec. This offer is limited to one order per household. All orders subject to approval. Credit or debit balances in a customer's account(s) may be offset by any other outstanding balance owed by or to the customer. Please allow 4 to 6 weeks for delivery. Offer available while quantities last.

Your Privacy: Harlequin Books is committed to protecting your privacy. Our Privacy Policy is available online at www.eHarlequin.com or upon request from the Reader Service. From time to time we make our lists of customers available to reputable third parties who may have a product or service of interest to you. If you would prefer we not share your name and address, please check here. ☐

HP09R

You've read the book, now see how the story began...in the hit game!

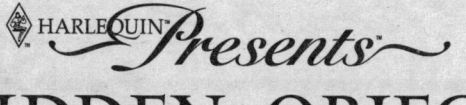

HARLEQUIN™ *Presents*™

HIDDEN OBJECT OF DESIRE

*The first-ever Harlequin romance series game
for your PC or Mac™ computer*

The feud that fuels the passion in the Royal House of Karedes all began when an assassin set his eyes on the Prince of Aristo. Dive into the drama to find out how it all began in an amazing interactive game based on your favorite books!

Hidden Object of Desire is now available online at

www.bigfishgames.com/harlequin

Try the game for free!

Brought to you by Harlequin and Big Fish Games

I ♥ HARLEQUIN *Presents*

BROUGHT TO YOU BY FANS OF
HARLEQUIN PRESENTS.

We are its editors and authors
and biggest fans—and we'd
love to hear from YOU!

Subscribe today to our online blog at
www.iheartpresents.com